Maggie Moore

and the Growing Surprise

Saturday, 6th September

School starts back in two days and I have a BIG problem. At the end of last term, Mrs Perkins, who's going to be our new teacher, sent out an email asking everyone to bring in a holiday souvenir when we start back in September.

I looked up the word souvenir on the computer and it said: 'A special object that is kept as a reminder of a place or event'.

Apparently, we're going to have to show our souvenir to the rest of the class, and there's even going to be a prize for the best presentation.

I think this is pretty unfair as some people, like my friend Mandy, go on really exciting holidays to America and will be able to take in something amazing, whereas I only ever go camping in the middle of nowhere and there aren't that many exciting souvenirs available in a wet field.

During my camping trip with my mum, dad and younger brother, Joppin, I did look for something that may be suitable. I found some damp twigs and a few pebbles, but nothing that seemed good enough to show to the class.

So here I am with two days to go until school starts back and I have no souvenir. Oh dear! I'm getting a bit desperate now and I'm considering taking in a random object from under my bed. I had a look but there are just old toys under there. There's a glove rabbit (a toy rabbit that Mum made out of a pair of gloves), but it doesn't really look like something you'd find on a camping trip, and the other toys, such as the pull-along turtle, are a bit babyish.

'Can we go on a different holiday next year?' I asked Mum as I looked in the kitchen cupboard for something to take in. 'It would be good to try something that wasn't camping.'

'Yes, we can stay in a fancy hotel somewhere,' she said, 'if you pay for it.'

Hmmmm, perhaps I'll try and make some money during the next year. I would love to go and stay in a hotel somewhere. That would be totally amazing. I can picture it now – watching TV in bed, ordering room service, and not having to go outside to go to the toilet. BLISS!

Sunday, 7th September

I rang my best friend Holly today and asked her what she was taking in.

'Oh, just a little straw donkey from Spain,' she said. 'How about you?'

'Oh, um, it's a surprise,' I said nervously, wishing I knew. After lunch I went into the garden to look for inspiration. All I could find was a tiny dried-up acorn. I reluctantly picked it up and put it in my pocket, just in case I can't find anything better before tomorrow.

Monday, 8th September
FIRST DAY BACK AT SCHOOL

I didn't find anything better so I had to take in the dried-up acorn. As soon as I got into the playground I saw Holly carrying an enormous straw donkey under her arm. It was nearly as big as her and it wore a straw hat and a scarf made from brightly-coloured pompoms.

'That's amazing!' I shrieked as I ran over to her.

'His name is Jacobi,' she said. 'It was so funny carrying him through the airport with everyone looking. So where's your souvenir?'

'Oh, um, I'm keeping it hidden so it will be a big surprise,' I said nervously.

'Ohhhhh,' said Holly, 'I can't wait to find out what it is. I love surprises.'

Just then Mandy walked over, her super-smooth long blonde hair shining in the sun. She was wearing these brown boots with loads of tassels hanging off them.

'Like my cowboy boots?' she asked. 'They're from America... so I'm wearing my souvenir.'

'They're nice,' I said.

Mandy stamped up and down a bit to make the tassels fly about then she noticed Holly's donkey.

'I love it,' she said as she started to stroke the donkey's head. 'What have you brought in, Maggie?'

I felt myself going red.

'Maggie's item is going to be a huge surprise, so no one can know until later,' said Holly.

'I can't wait,' said Mandy.

Quentin, the biggest show-off in the school, came over to us. 'Your souvenirs are absolutely rubbish,' he said, looking at Mandy's boots and poking Jacobi in the nose. 'There's no point anyone trying to win the prize for the best presentation as mine will definitely win, just wait and see. It's going to blow your minds.'

The bell rang and we all rushed into our new classroom. We were hoping to see our other friend Sarah before the bell went, but she was late and we had to hurry in without her.

Everyone was carrying some strange item or another. Quentin walked in followed by two men who were carrying a huge box that looked extremely heavy. Holly and I raised our eyebrows as they placed it next to his desk.

As we sat down everyone was chatting and looking at each other's items. Jake had a rather strange plastic toilet that turned out to be a moneybox and Peter had some rather strange leather shorts from Germany.

After about five minutes Mrs Perkins walked in and everyone stopped talking. Mrs Perkins is quite a serious lady with a very pointy nose, short black hair, and glasses that look like they have yellow lenses.

'It's not the lenses, she's got yellow eyes,' whispered Jake as she took her position at the front.

7

'Hello, my new class,' she said. 'I can see you've all brought something in. Well done!' She picked up a model of the Eiffel Tower from big Claire's desk at the front. 'We're going to have so much fun talking about your items. In fact, we're not just going to talk about what you've brought in, we're going to integrate them into all sorts of different pieces of work this year.'

I wasn't quite sure what she meant but I felt a little nervous as I touched the acorn in my pocket.

'What's the prize for the best presentation?' asked Quentin, patting his box.

'The prize is a beautiful item that I found on my holiday. You'll have to wait and see what it is.'

Suddenly, there was a clattering noise at the door and everyone turned round to see Sarah with a huge duck-shaped rubber ring around her waist.

'Excuse me, sorry I'm late,' she said as she struggled past everyone and walked over to the last empty seat at the other side of the room.

'Where have you been?' asked Mrs Perkins.

'Oh, the Bathing Museum.'

'I mean, why are you late?'

'Sorry. It took longer than expected to blow up Bill.' Everyone giggled as she sat down with the duck still around her middle, her round glasses all steamed up and her cheeks very flushed.

8

No one got a chance to do a souvenir presentation in the morning as we did a huge spelling test; it was mega hard and even included the word 'encyclopaedia', which only Quentin got right. Once the test was done, Mrs Perkins spent about an hour telling us how she used to be a journalist who wrote articles in a famous newspaper. Apparently, she used to pretend to be a baddie so she could find out about crimes and then write about them for the paper. 'It's called undercover journalism,' she said. It all sounded quite exciting but sort of dangerous.

After lunch we went back into the classroom and Mrs Perkins said we'd have time to see a few of the souvenir presentations. Mandy was called up first and she strode up to the front, where she put on some music via her new MP3 player. She then started doing line-dancing moves, the tassels on her boots flying about with every step.

'That was a type of American dancing,' she said after giving a deep bow. 'But that's not all I've got,' she said, before digging into her bag and getting out all sorts of other things, including:

A t-shirt with an American flag printed on it
A cowboy hat
A dreamcatcher
A bag of coins

and 32 rubbers (or erasers as she's started calling them [all different shapes]).

'Okay, Mandy, thank you,' said Mrs Perkins. 'That was a good, confident presentation,' she added.

Mandy flipped the cowboy hat onto her head and sashayed back to her seat.

Quentin put his hand up. 'Can I go next please, Mrs Perkins? I have to take my souvenir home tonight and I don't know if I'll be allowed to bring it in again tomorrow.'

'Very well,' she said, looking at the rather large box. Quentin jumped up and tried to move it, but he was struggling so much that Mrs Perkins had to help him push it to the front of the room.

Everyone watched in silence as he began to remove the heavy brown tape that sealed the box. Suddenly, a strange, long, high-pitched sound came out of it. Everyone screamed and a few of the girls at the front jumped up. Then a woman burst up out of the box as it opened. She was wearing a kilt and holding bagpipes. She started playing a terrible high-pitched tune as everyone stared in disbelief. It sounded awful and people were trying not to wince. After she finished she did a curtsey, and everyone clapped politely.

'Thank you,' said Mrs Perkins, looking alarmed. She stared at the bagpipe woman. 'Who are you?' she asked.

'I'm Quentin's mum,' the woman replied, stepping out of the box and smoothing down her kilt. Quentin then did a talk about Scottish history while his mum stood there looking a bit embarrassed. 'That'll be a hard presentation to beat,' Quentin's mum said as she stumbled out of the room carrying the bagpipes.

'Very unusual,' said Mr Perkins. 'So your mother has been crouching in a box for four hours?'

Quentin nodded proudly. 'Five actually, she's been in there since before breakfast.' Mrs Perkins scratched her head.

Big Claire was next and she talked about going up the Eiffel Tower. Everyone seemed to have a lot to say about the souvenirs. I decided that bringing in the acorn was a terrible idea, and I hoped I wouldn't have to do my presentation until another day. I knew I had to find something else as soon as I got home. I wondered if I could take in a tent or a camping chair. It had to be something big. I was so busy thinking about it I didn't hear my name being called out.

'Maggie?'

Holly nudged me. 'It's your turn,' she whispered. 'I can't wait to find out what it is.'

11

The blood drained from my face as I slowly went to the front.

'Come on, Maggie, have a bit of oomph,' said Mrs Perkins.

I stood there, unable to speak.

'What have you got to show us then?' asked Mrs Perkins.

I put my shaking hand into my pocket and took out the acorn, keeping it hidden in my fingers.

'Come on, don't be shy, show us,' said Mrs Perkins, starting to sound annoyed. I opened my hand to reveal the small shrunken acorn. Everybody fell about laughing.

'No laughing, please,' said Mrs Perkins crossly.

'Um,' I muttered quietly, 'this is my souvenir from camping at Brundel Forest.'

'And why is it special to you?' asked Mrs Perkins.

'Well...,' I began, '... it's... part of nature and it could grow into a huge tree.'

'Ahaaa!' said Mrs Perkins as she stood up and clapped her hands together excitedly. She ran up to the whiteboard and wrote, 'Mighty oaks from little acorns grow' in wild writing.

'Go on,' she said, suddenly looking at me intently. I decided to carry on along the same lines, as Mrs Perkins seemed to like it. I pointed to the acorn.

'Yes, in here is a tree, well it could be a tree, and

12

that tree could grow acorns that could become more trees.' I glanced at Mrs Perkins, who was nodding eagerly. 'So,' I said, holding it up, 'this acorn could create thousands of trees.'

'And how does it tie in with your camping trip?' she asked.

'Well… camping reminds us of living with nature and the acorn is a part of nature.'

Mrs Perkins clapped again. 'I love it,' she said. Everyone seemed very surprised that Mrs Perkins was being so positive, especially Quentin, whose mouth was hanging open. 'Amazing,' she continued. 'It reminds me of a quote by George Bernard Shaw.' She then rubbed out everything on the whiteboard and wrote: 'Think of the fierce energy concentrated in the acorn! You bury it in the ground and it explodes into an oak.' She spun round, her eyes twinkling and a broad smile on her face. She patted me on the back as I went back to my seat. I'm starting to quite like Mrs Perkins.

Quentin came up to me after school. 'That acorn was absolutely rubbish,' he said, 'as if that would ever win. I don't think anyone can beat my mum playing the bagpipes.' He then rushed off, nose in the air, to find his mum, who was waiting in the car.

'Don't listen to Quentin. Your presentation was brilliant,' said Holly as we left the playground.

13

'Yes,' added Mandy as she caught us up, 'you managed to make something really rubbish sound sort of good.'

Tuesday, 9th September

More people did presentations this morning, including Holly (accompanied by Jacobi the donkey) and Sarah (accompanied by Bill the duck). At playtime we took the souvenirs outside and got the duck to sit nicely on the donkey's back. No one could think of anything to do with the acorn – well, no one except Jake, but I didn't really like his idea of putting my acorn into his toilet moneybox.

Jacobi the donkey was particularly popular with everyone and lots of people came over to see it. Jake really liked the scarf of pompoms around its neck.

'How much for a blue pompom?' he asked.

'I'm not cutting a pompom off Jacobi's scarf,' said Holly, hugging the donkey protectively.

'I'll give you one pound,' he said.

'I'll give you one pound for a red one,' said Peter.

'I'll think about it,' said Holly.

Thursday, 11th September

'Now that you've all finished talking about your items,' said Mrs Perkins today, 'we'll have a look at their shape, and then draw them.'

'But my mum isn't here to draw,' whined Quentin.

'Well, you'll have to draw her from memory.'

'It's far from ideal, but I'll try,' he said, sighing deeply.

I put my acorn in front of me and got my pencil and paper ready.

'You only have one hour to complete this task,' said Mrs Perkins.

ONE HOUR!?!! To draw a tiny acorn!?!!

I finished my drawing in 20 seconds and sat there looking at it, wondering what I'd do for the next 59 minutes and 40 seconds. I decided to shade it in really slowly, but after I'd done that I still had 58 minutes to go.

To appear busy, I continued adding shading to the acorn picture for the full hour. At the end of the lesson it looked like a black hole in the middle of the page with lots of smudges around it.

I looked at other people's detailed drawings of donkeys, towers, snow globes, and all sorts of other amazing things. Even Quentin's picture of his mum playing the bagpipes was quite good.

I was really embarrassed about my drawing and I kept my hand over it as much as I could, which made it look even more smudged and terrible.

At the end of the lesson Mrs Perkins collected in all the drawings. I managed to slide mine in at the bottom of the pile. I hope she never notices it.

Friday, 12th September

I walked into the classroom today and stopped dead in my tracks. There, covering one whole wall, were all the drawings we'd done yesterday. My smudged acorn picture was right in the middle. It looked like a two-year-old had spilt something in the middle of a page. To make matters worse, all the best drawings seemed to be surrounding it.

'As you can see,' said Mrs Perkins at the start of the lesson, 'the drawings are up and I think they're very good.'

'Is that a squashed bug in the middle?' asked Peter, pointing at mine. I held my breath.

'This one?' she asked, touching my picture. 'No, it's one of my favourites. It shows the condensed intensity of the acorn.' She looked at me. 'Do these paler marks coming out of the acorn represent the potential power trying to get out?' she asked.

'Um… yes,' I said as I looked up and nodded.

Saturday, 13th September

Dad's made a monkey bar climbing frame for the garden, and Joppin and I spent ages practising swinging across the bars and hanging upside down on the trapeze he'd added.

Dad's really into making things and this is one of his better ideas.

Sometimes I quite enjoy playing with my brother Joppin even though he's a couple of years younger than me. We do argue now and then, but generally he's not too bad. Today we got on quite well and even made a den behind the shed.

Monday, 15th September

Mrs Perkins came into the classroom carrying a small box. 'I've decided on a winner for the best presentation,' she said, placing the box on her desk.

Everyone started chatting about who should win, and Quentin began pointing at himself. I wasn't mentioned at all.

'Quiet, please.'

The room went very quiet as everyone looked at the plain brown package tied up with string. Mrs Perkins began walking back and forth.

'This prize doesn't go to the person with the most expensive or the biggest souvenir,' she said. 'This prize goes to the person who thought deeply, the person who saw beyond herself.' She paused then said, 'Maggie, please come to the front.'

I looked up, wondering why my name was being

called out. I went to the front, thinking I was going to be asked to hand the box to the winner.

'Who do I give it to?' I asked.

'You're the winner, Maggie, well done!' she said.

Everyone started complaining.

'That's not fair, hers was the worst,' said Jake.

'Maggie's presentation was absolutely rubbish,' added Quentin furiously.

'Mine was better,' said Claire.

I stood there looking down. I knew my presentation was pretty bad but all the comments were extremely embarrassing.

'You've done really well,' said Mrs Perkins, looking at me. 'You're a deep thinker.' I picked up the box and went back to my desk. I kept my head down because my cheeks were bright red and I was trying to avoid looking at anyone.

At playtime Quentin flew over to me. 'Your terrible presentation about a dead acorn shouldn't have won. This isn't the end of it. My mum will be complaining so don't open your prize yet,' he shouted, before storming off.

'Ha ha,' said Holly, 'no one can believe you won, but I'm glad you did.'

'At least Quentin didn't win,' said Mandy, 'although I do think my presentation was a bit better than yours, no offence.'

'Well, are you going to open it?' asked Holly.

'No, I think I'll open it on my own tonight,' I said. 'I'll let you know what it is tomorrow.'

LATER

I raced into my room and sat on my bed with the box in front of me. My heart was beating fast as I untied the string really carefully and lifted the cardboard flaps. (I was being extra careful in case I had to repackage it for the real winner later.) I opened the box and peered in. As soon as I realised what it was my heart sank. It was a plain grey pebble with a note next to it. I unfolded the note and read it. It said: 'The pleasure of winning is better than the prize itself.'

Hmmmmmm, I'm not sure about that. I lifted the pebble out, hoping it was something more than just a pebble, perhaps a remote control robot pebble or a gold nugget painted grey. But no, it was just a pebble. I dropped it back in the box and shoved it under my bed.

Tuesday, 16th September

'Well,' said Holly, running up to me this morning, 'what was the prize?' Quentin sidled over to us, keen to hear the answer.

I couldn't bring myself to tell them it was just a plain pebble. 'Um, it's an amazing fossil,' I said shakily.

'I collect fossils,' said Quentin. 'I am so getting my mum in to complain to Mrs Foley.' Mrs Foley is the head teacher and would probably be allowed to overrule Mrs Perkins' decision, which is rather worrying.

My stomach turned over. If Quentin is given the prize instead of me, he'll find out it's only a pebble.

'Can you bring it in to show us?' asked Holly.

'Yeah, another day,' I said vaguely.

Friday, 19th September

Luckily, nothing was mentioned about Quentin's mum complaining, so hopefully that means I won't have to hand the pebble over. The girls keep asking me to bring the fossil in, but I keep saying I've forgotten it. I really wish I'd just said it was a pebble, as now I feel very, very worried about being found out. I don't know why I didn't say. I was just so embarrassed that the prize was so bad.

P.S. Holly sold one of Jacobi's pompoms to Jake for £1 today!

Monday, 22nd September
SCHOOL NEWSPAPER

I'm so excited because our class is going to be making a school newspaper. The first edition has to be ready by the end of October, so we have about six weeks to do it.

The class was split into groups (I'm with Holly, Mandy and Sarah – hooray!). Each group has been given a different job. Our group is doing news.

We have to find some news stories for the paper, which must include some writing and a picture.

'The best news story can go on the front,' said Mrs Perkins as she came over to our group, 'so you need a good headline and an eye-catching photo or drawing. 'You'll have to decide on the best story yourselves because I want the paper to be all your own work. In fact, I'm not going to look at it until it's published.'

This is all quite exciting, although none of us could think of any good stories.

Jake, Peter and a couple of the other boys are going to be doing jokes and quizzes, Claire and her group are designing the title and illustrations, and another group is making a comic strip page. Quentin is running a competition and doing some sort of maths page.

I kind of wish our group was doing the comic strip page, but Mrs Perkins said that we have to do the jobs she's given us.

We might be doing another edition next term (if this one is a success), so hopefully we'll get a chance to do comic strips or illustrations then.

At lunchtime we sat at the picnic table in the playground. 'So who can think of a news story?' asked Mandy.

'I guess it has to be something to do with the school as it's a school newspaper,' said Holly.

'We could do something about my new cowboy boots,' said Mandy.

'I'm not sure that's newsworthy enough,' said Holly. Mandy looked away, frowning slightly.

Wednesday, 24th September

'Perhaps we could feature your fossil prize in the newspaper,' said Holly after lunch today.

'Nah, that's old news,' I said, my heart racing.

'You're right, we need BIG news,' said Holly, 'but nothing really exciting ever seems to happen around here.'

Jake and Peter were giggling behind a tree nearby. I shuffled over to listen in. 'Yeah,' said Jake, 'let's have a quiz where every single answer is the word toilet.' I shuffled away again.

Thursday, 25th September

Holly sold one more pompom today. She says that it's the last one she'll sell as Jacobi's scarf is starting to look a bit sparse. It's given me an idea for a business though. After all, I need to make some money as Mum said I need to pay if we are to go on a better holiday next year. I invited Holly round for tea on Saturday to discuss my plan further.

Friday, 26th September
FOSSIL WORRY

Oh no! Holly's coming round tomorrow and she might ask to look at the fossil! I'd forgotten all about it when I invited her.

Luckily, I have a plan. I got the pebble out from under my bed earlier and drew a fossily shape on it with a black pen. Then I blotted the ink to make it look really old. I think it kind of looks very slightly fossily. Well, if I show it to her really quickly, she might be fooled. Eeeeeek!

Saturday, 27th September
HOLLY

It was quite sunny when Holly arrived so we played in the garden for a while. After going on the monkey bars we played this game on the trampoline called 'crack the egg'. First Holly rolled into a ball in the middle of the trampoline then I jumped around her trying to make her come out of the ball shape. It was quite fun.

After a while Mum called us in for tea. We had pizza, dough balls and carrot sticks and finished the meal with cookie dough ice cream. Yumalicious!

After tea I showed Holly this website I'd found that was about how to make woollen pompoms. All you need is cardboard, wool and scissors. Luckily, my mum had all these things.

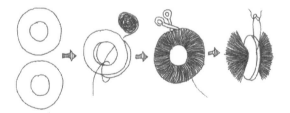

'So, to make money, we can make pompoms and sell them,' I said.

'Brilliant idea!' said Holly as we rushed to get everything.

'Let's sell them for £1 each,' I said as I began cutting circle shapes out of cardboard.

We were very excited and started making the pompoms straight away. Luckily, because Mum is really into anything like sewing, knitting or craft she had a whole box full of different wools. I chose blue and green while Holly chose black and glittery.

It took quite a long time but we made two very nice pompoms ready to sell next week.

We were just about to sit down and watch a TV show called *Art in Unusual Places* when Holly said the dreaded words, 'Oh, Maggie, can I see your fossil?'

'Ummmm, yeeeees, I'll go and get it,' I said, my legs shaking as I got to the stairs. I decided that a quick show without taking it out of the box was my best option.

Things didn't go quite as planned though. As I did my fleeting show Holly grabbed the stone and examined it carefully. She even licked her finger and rubbed off some of the ink!!!!

'Oh, Maggie, I hate to have to tell you this,' she said, looking me straight in the eye, 'but I think it could be a fake.' I pretended to look shocked. 'Look, the fossil bit rubs off,' she said, licking her finger again and rubbing off even more of the ink.

'Oh well, never mind,' I said quickly, putting the stone back in the box.

'This could be the big news story,' said Holly jumping up. 'Teacher gives a fake fossil as a prize.'

'Um, perhaps... if we can't find any better stories,' I said, knowing that we now HAVE to find better stories.

Monday, 29th September
HOLIDAY FUND = £1

I sold my pompom to Peter and received £1. This is an excellent start for the business, which I've called 'Pompoms Forever'. I've made some business cards and I'm going to make another pompom tonight.

I've started a holiday money fund where I will collect all the money I earn this year. I really hope I can get enough for the hotel break I have in mind.

Tuesday, 30th September

I looked around the playground, desperate to come up with an idea for a good story for the newspaper. After all, I definitely don't want the 'fossil' to be featured. 'Okay,' I said, sitting at the picnic table with the others after lunch. 'Let's do a world record for the most people to fit under this picnic table, and that can be one of the news stories.'

'Hmmmmm, do you think it's exciting enough for the paper?' asked Mandy.

'Better than nothing,' I said.

'Okay, we'll do it tomorrow and I'll bring in my camera,' said Sarah.

'But don't tell anyone,' said Holly. 'If someone finds out, they may get more people under it and ruin our record.'

It was agreed that it would all be top secret.

Wednesday, 1st October

At playtime we all went and casually sat at the picnic table. Mr Blott, the Year One teacher, was on duty, so we waited until he wasn't looking then one by one we slid under the table.

Soon we were all squashed under and Sarah got out her camera. She was just about to take the photo when Mr Blott, who clearly hadn't seen us, came and sat at the table. We all froze, not sure what to do.

Mr Blott then took off his shoe and started rubbing his foot through his sock. What was very alarming was that his foot was right next to my face. I grimaced and looked at Holly, who was trying not to laugh. After another minute he put his hand into his sock and began rubbing again. 'Oh, I hate fungal infections,' he mumbled to himself as he put his shoe back on and walked off. Once he was out of sight we all crawled out. Mandy was laughing away. I was still feeling a little strange after being so close to the whole foot rubbing thing.

'Well, did you get the photo of us all under the table?' asked Holly.

'No, I didn't want Mr Blott to hear the click,' said Sarah.

'What's a fungal infection?' I asked.

'I don't know but fungus is definitely something to do with mushrooms,' said Mandy.

Our eyes opened wide as we imagined mushrooms growing out of Mr Blott's toes. EEEEEEEEEEEK!

We all looked at each other in shock.

Just then the bell went and we had to go back into school.

Thursday, 2nd October

We had to work on the newspaper this afternoon so we all got into our groups. We decided not to do an article about Mr Blott's fungal infection, even though Holly said she had a really good idea for a drawing. (Which would include mushrooms growing out of a foot and an elf sitting on a toe. Ewwwwwww!)

'It's just too gross,' said Mandy.

'And I don't think we should embarrass Mr Blott,' said Sarah.

We also did some important planning and decided to go under the table again next week to try and get a good photo to accompany the world record story.

Saturday, 4th October

There was a removal van near our house today. A house down the street has been empty for a few months and it looks like someone's moving in. I watched out of my window, wondering who it could be. I was kind of hoping for some kids around my age, but I could just see an old man shuffling about.

Sunday, 5th October

I've now met the new neighbour as Mum made me go round with her to meet him. She took a jam jar of sugar with her. I have no idea why.

'Hello,' she said when he opened the door. He looked pretty old.

'Hello, can I help you?'

'We live down the road,' Mum said before introducing us.

'I'm Mr Alimo,' he said. Then there was a long silence.

'A present for you,' said Mum, giving him the sugar. He looked confused but took it.

'Thank you,' he said, shutting the door.

'Why did you give him a jar of sugar?' I asked as we returned home.

'Everyone knows that people need sugar when they move house,' she said.

In the afternoon Joppin and I rode our bikes up and down the street and I saw Mr Alimo in the front garden digging up the lawn.

'Hi, what are you doing?' I asked, stopping my bike near him.

'Getting rid of the grass,' he said. 'Grass is a waste of a garden - there are much better things to grow.'

Monday, 6th October

After taking the register Mrs Perkins asked us all to think about the souvenirs we'd brought in earlier in the term. I thought about my acorn, which now lived in my school tray and was looking more wrinkled than ever.

'I want you to do a piece of creative writing from the point of view of your souvenir,' she said.

Claire, who'd brought in a model of the Eiffel Tower, put her hand up. 'Do we have to pretend our souvenir is alive?' she asked.

'It's up to you. You can give it feelings or just talk about what happens inside it or write something from the point of view of the real Eiffel Tower. This is a creative writing challenge so be creative.'

I was really struggling to think of something to write and looked over at Holly. She'd written 'The Adventures of Jacobi' on her page and was scribbling away. I decided to write about the moment roots and shoots started coming out of the acorn. It was quite weird pretending I was an acorn under the ground and even weirder pretending a shoot was growing out of my body, but I kind of got into it (a bit).

At the end of the lesson a few people read out what they'd written. Quentin's was from the point of view of his mum and it was all about what a wonderful son she had. Hmmmmmm.

Jake also read his out, well he read half of it out then he had to be stopped because it was from the point of view of a toilet and every other sentence included the word wee or pee. YUK!

Saturday, 11th October

Mr Alimo has now dug up the whole of his front garden. We saw him planting something in the soil. 'Garlic!' he shouted as we walked past.

Sunday, 12th October

My dad, who is really into making things, is especially happy if he can make things out of other people's waste. This essentially means that a lot of our stuff is made out of rubbish.

Today we had to drive around in the car looking for skips with junk in them. Dad wants to make some garden furniture and he was looking for scrap wood. When he saw a skip outside a large house, he pulled up and rang the doorbell. Whoever lived there gave him the go-ahead and he started transferring an old door and four old toilet seats (eeeekyyuk!) into the car. There was also an old tyre so he threw that in too.

When we got home, he tied the tyre onto the monkey bars, which was really good. Joppin and I played on it for ages. Then he started turning the door into a garden table. After that something quite worrying happened. He began attaching legs to the toilet seats to make garden stools! This is mega embarrassing because sometimes my friends come round to play and I would be mortified if they saw toilet seat stools in the garden. Eeeeeeeek! I'll have to come up with a plan to get rid of them.

CREATIVE WRITING

'Imagine you could go inside your souvenir,' said Mrs Perkins today. 'What would it be like? Would there be another world? Would there be people? Would there be sounds? That is your creative writing challenge for today.'

I began writing my story about a world inside my acorn where tiny oak trees can talk and run about on their roots. It was quite good.

'I'm not sure this is appropriate,' said Quentin. 'I don't want to imagine I'm inside my mother, squashed in next to her kidney or something.'

'Um, well, do the bagpipes then, Quentin,' Mrs Perkins replied.

'Shall I go into Jacobi through the mouth?' asked Holly.

Mrs Perkins sighed. 'It's up to you.'

'Can I be in the toilet when it's flushed?' asked Jake.

Mrs Perkins went out to do some photocopying.

ASSEMBLY

In the afternoon we had assembly. Mrs Foley, the head teacher, marched into the hall and stood at the front.

'Autumn,' she said, 'is a time to reflect and enjoy the fruits of our labour. It's the season where nature gives us glorious views and colours. My garden is looking beautiful. It's full of berries, sculptures and stunning autumn trees. And I have some exciting news.' She paused while we all wondered what it was. 'My own garden is going to be featured on the TV show *Best Autumn Garden*,' she continued. 'This just shows what can be achieved with hard work and determination. I really hope lots of you will watch it and perhaps even phone in to vote for your favourite garden.'

Everyone was quite impressed that Mrs Foley's garden would be on such a popular show. At playtime it was the talk of the playground.

'My dad always watches it,' said Sarah.

'I watch it every year. I can't believe it,' added Holly.

'All the gardens on it are amazing so Mrs Foley's garden must be pretty good,' said Claire.

Wednesday, 15th October

When no one was looking, we all squashed in under the picnic table and managed to get quite a good photo. RESULT!!! That will be a good picture to go with the 'Most people ever under the school picnic table' story for the newspaper.

Luckily, Mr Blott stayed at the other side of the playground today so there were no feet issues.

'What are you doing under there?' asked Quentin, walking over.

'Um, looking for my pencil,' said Holly.

'You lot are very strange,' he said, walking off.

After school Holly was waiting for her older sister to pick her up. I waited with her just outside the staffroom window, which was slightly open. We could hear Mrs Foley talking inside. I peeked in and saw that she was the only person in there and that she was on her phone.

'Yes, it's been a very difficult time,' said Mrs Foley as she paced up and down. 'I mean I just didn't know what to do with the body.'

Holly and I stared at each other. I felt all the hairs on the back of my neck stand up.

'I was going to burn it,' she continued, 'but I just buried it in my garden in the end.' Then there was a long pause. 'Yes, I'll tell you more when I see you,' she said, before putting the phone in her pocket.

We ran away from the staffroom as fast as we could and waited in the street, panting.

'Do you think she murdered someone?' whispered Holly.

'I don't know, but it's not normal to bury a body in your garden.'

We decided to tell Mandy and Sarah about it the next day.

All evening I just kept thinking about Mrs Foley, wondering what she'd done, who she'd buried, and why.

Thursday, 16th October

'This could be the big news story,' said Mandy after we told her what we'd heard.

'I don't know, I think we should tell the police,' said Sarah.

'Noooooooo,' said Mandy, 'this is a scoop for our newspaper. We'll be the very first people to report it. We'll be famous for uncovering it! We'll be proper investigating reporters.'

We nervously agreed to keep it secret until the paper was out.

Every time I saw Mrs Foley I felt a chill run down my spine.

Friday, 17th October

'Who wants to come to my house for lunch on Saturday?' Mandy asked this morning. We all agreed that we'd like to go.

'That's good news,' she said, 'because I've found out where Mrs Foley lives and it's really near my house. Let's go and see if we can spot any fresh digging in her garden.'

 'But we can't just go into her garden,' said Sarah.

'Yeah, it's fine,' said Mandy. 'I've been past it before and I'm pretty sure it's on a corner where you can see into the garden from the street'.

Phew!

Saturday, 18th October

'I'll pick you up at two,' said Dad as he dropped me off at Mandy's big stone house. I was the first to arrive so Mandy and I played on the computer until the others arrived.

We had sushi for lunch, which was kind of strange but weirdly quite nice. It was rice wrapped in seaweed with bits of raw fish in the middle. For dessert we had hot chocolate pudding with custard. YUM!

After lunch we told Mandy's dad that we were just popping out to the park, which is quite near her house.

'Okay, as long as you all stick together,' he said as he started the washing up.

Mandy had drawn a map and we followed it until we came to Mrs Foley's house. We knew it was hers straight away because her funny yellow car was in the drive.

I started biting my nails and felt a shiver run through me. I wondered what would happen if there was a hand sticking up out of a pile of soil.

We peered over the garden wall but we could just see a nice garden with neat hedges, curvy sculptures and lots of flowers. We then saw a spade leaning against a wall.

'That spade is proof,' said Mandy. 'We'd better get out of here before we're seen.' We turned and ran towards the park.

When we got back to Mandy's house later, we all went and sat on the beanbags in her room.

'So who do you think she's buried?' asked Mandy.

We came up with all sorts of possible ideas. Holly's convinced it's one of the teachers who left suddenly last term, but I think she left to have a baby.

It's so weird because I just can't imagine Mrs Foley doing anything bad. In fact, she's always talking about how important it is to do the right thing.

Monday, 20th October

There's not long to go until the newspaper articles need to be ready so we spent quite a lot of today working on our various jobs and have come up with a headline for our main article: 'Head Teacher Buries Body in Garden'.

'Ten days to go until everything is going to be sent to the printers,' said Mrs Perkins, walking around the room. Mandy quickly covered our pages with her arms.

'Thank goodness Mrs Perkins isn't going to read anything until the paper's ready,' whispered Mandy.

Wednesday, 22nd October

Holly decided to do the artwork for the buried body article today. She drew a picture of a pile of soil with a little hand sticking out of it. It looked really funny. We also worked a bit more on the writing...

Head Teacher Buries Body in Garden

Does a mystery head teacher at Weatherbrook School have something to hide?

Secret sources overheard her saying that she has buried a body in her garden.

'I'm worried we could get into trouble,' said Sarah.

'No,' said Mandy, 'if there's a body in her garden, she's the one who will get into trouble. We're just helping to solve a possible crime. Plus we'll probably get an award for uncovering it.'

'And,' said Holly, 'we haven't actually mentioned her name.'

Saturday, 25th October

Mum was reading a camping magazine tonight, which has reminded me that I need to make some more money to add to the holiday fund.

I checked the Travel Hotel website and the prices seem to start at about £40 a night, so I've decided I need to get a move on and make some more pompoms to sell. As it's nearly Halloween I've made pumpkin pompoms and added black felt features. They look really good and I spent quite a long time making six of them.

Monday, 27th October

Hooray, I managed to sell three pompoms today!!

HOLIDAY FUND = £4

YIPPPEEEEEE!

Tuesday, 28th October

This morning we had the chance to finish our newspaper articles. We realised that although it was amazing, we'd only finished one story.

We worked on our other story about our new world record.

Amazing World Record Set at Weatherbrook School

Four people have managed to fit under the Weatherbrook School picnic table. This is a great achievement and congratulations go to all those involved.

'Pretty good,' said Holly as she put the photo under it.

Wednesday, 29th October

I sold two more pompoms today. Claire bought them and said she was going to make them into earrings for Halloween.

HOLIDAY FUND = £6

Thursday, 30th October

We put our articles and pictures into the big envelope to be sent to the printers. We were very careful to make sure nobody saw them. Luckily, Holly was in charge of checking the page order and layout so no one other than us knows about the buried body. The paper will be ready on 5th November. I'm nervous about what will happen when everyone reads it.

Friday, 31st October
HALLOWEEN

4 p.m.

Mandy, Sarah and I are going round to Holly's house tonight so that we can go trick or treating. I'm going to be dressing up as the Incredible Hulk. Just in case you don't know who the Hulk is, he's this guy who goes very green and very big when he's angry. He grows so big that he ends up in ripped ragged clothes. I know that doesn't sound very Halloweenish, but I've got all the things I need to make the costume and I think I'm going to look rather good.

Mum has all these bags of old clothes lying around ready to sell in her eBay shop, and there's loads of green food colouring in the cupboard left over from when Mum tried to make a green Christmas tree cake last year.

TIME TO GO GREEN

I've cut up some trousers and a shirt to be the Hulk's ripped clothes, so all that's left to do now is to go green.

I haven't told Mum about the green food colouring plan, as there's a small chance she might not let me use it. I'm just going to sneak into the garden and apply it when no one's looking.

20 MINUTES LATER

It worked!!!!!! I am now officially green! I took all the green food colouring I could find plus a sponge

44

and bucket into the garden.

I applied the bright green liquid to my face, neck, arms and lower legs and it looks really good.

I don't quite have the muscles of the Hulk so I've tied the two leftover pompoms to my arms and they sort of look like big muscles. (Well, they don't really, but I'm going to wear them anyway.)

I'm so excited about going to Holly's now!

LATER

I put on the ripped clothes and looked in the mirror. I looked very much like the Hulk and I couldn't believe how green I was. I went to show Mum, who covered her mouth with both hands.

'Well, let's hope it washes off by Monday,' she said.

'I'm sure it will.'

'You know it's the class photos?'

I'd forgotten all about the class photos, but I'm sure it'll come off quite easily.

Joppin came in dressed as a ghost in Dad's white pyjamas. When he saw me, his mouth dropped open. 'I want to be the Hulk,' he said. Then he went off with Mum to look for some old clothes to rip up. Sadly, there was no green food colouring left so he had to be a pale pink Hulk.

Dad drove me round to Holly's house. 'You're GREEEEEEEEEEEEEEEEEN!' shrieked Holly as she opened the door. Everyone ran over to have a look.

'That's amazing!' said Mandy, touching my arm. 'Your skin really looks like it's green... um, what are you?'

'I'm the Hulk,' I said. Mandy looked at me blankly. 'You know, the guy who goes big and green when he's angry?'

'No, but you look good anyway,' she said.

Mandy was a glamorous witch with a black-and-orange dress and sparkly tights. Holly wore a floor-length black velvet dress, vampire teeth and a large upturned collar, and Sarah wore a strange flat box with numbers on it.

'I'm a calculator,' said Sarah proudly, giving us a twirl. Holly and I started laughing and saying how scared we were.

Holly's mum had made some special Halloween snacks and we tucked into our eyeball buns and sausage fingers (complete with celery fingernails). After that we went out trick or treating. An old lady opened the very first door we knocked on. She smiled at us. 'Oh what a lovely frog,' she said to me, leaning in closely to examine my face. 'That is clever. How did you get your eyes to go all beady?'

I smiled politely, feeling my cheeks flush. Luckily, because of my green face no one noticed I was blushing. She gave each of us a lolly.

Everyone started laughing as we walked away. 'Do I look like a frog?' I asked.

'Nooooooo, she's just being silly,' said Holly. We went to another house. A man with two young boys opened the door. 'Look, a frog!' shouted one of the boys, pointing at me.

We went to several more houses and got loads of sweets, which we started eating as soon as we got back to Holly's house.

We then all squashed onto the sofa to watch a scary film. Well, it wasn't that scary. It was about a puppy who decided to become a wizard. Sarah couldn't sit down properly in her calculator costume so she lay across the top us and we kept pressing the buttons during the film.

Saturday, 1st November

I had a long bath today. I used about half a bottle of bubble bath... and I'm

STILL GREEN!

I scrubbed myself with Mum's special exfoliation sponge... but I'm

STILL GREEN!

I even tried using washing-up liquid... but I'm

STILL GREEN!

I'm now starting to get very worried about Monday, especially as it's the class photos.

Oh noooooooo!

Monday, 3rd November

I was crouched over my cornflakes trying to hide my face.

Joppin grinned. 'I'm glad there was no green food colouring left for me,' he said.

'Never mind, Maggie,' said Mum. 'It doesn't look that bad.' I knew this was a complete lie as I'd looked in the mirror and was bright, bright green.

'Can I miss school?' I asked, holding my hand over my face.

'Oh no, of course not,' said Mum.

I looked down as I entered the playground. I remembered what the old lady had said about me looking like a frog and I felt like hiding.

'You're still green!' said Holly as she ran over to me.

'I won't come off,' I whispered.

'Oh dear,' said Holly. 'Let's nip to the loo and see if we can sort it out.'

'I've tried everything.'

Suddenly, Quentin came over. When he saw me, he started laughing. 'That is the funniest thing I've ever seen,' he stammered, before running off to tell everyone.

Holly and I rushed into the toilets. She started scrubbing my face with a soap-covered paper towel, but it soon became obvious that it wouldn't make any difference.

'I know,' she said, rushing into one of the cubicles. She came out with a handful of white toilet paper. She ran a piece under the tap then slapped it onto my face, pressing it down. 'That covers it up,' she said. I let her apply about four more pieces but it made me look really strange, like my skin was coming off.

'I'm just going to have to spend the day green,' I said.

The photographer asked me to stand at the back. Then she pulled me back even further so I was standing about two metres behind everyone else. This was very embarrassing, especially as I saw several people trying not to laugh.

On top of this, Quentin started following me about at playtime asking me questions. 'What's the difference between Maggie and a chicken?' he said.

'I don't know,' I sighed.

'They're both green, oh, except the chicken,'

He was getting a rather annoying so Holly and I went and stood by Mr Winters, the teacher who was on playtime duty. Mr Winters looked at me and giggled, 'are you a green elf?' he said.

Tuesday, 4th November

Luckily, the green has faded quite a lot and this morning I was only slightly green. Unfortunately, my eyebrows were still very green and at breakfast Joppin kept chasing me, saying he was collecting caterpillars. Not very funny!

After lunch Mrs Perkins reminded us that the school newspaper would be back from the printers the next day. With Halloween and the whole being green thing we'd forgotten all about the school newspaper. A tingle ran through me as I realised that the following day everyone would know about the body in Mrs Foley's garden!!!

Wednesday, 5th November
THE SCHOOL NEWSPAPER IS OUT

OH NO!

OH NO!

OH NO!

When we got to school today, we all sat down as usual. Everyone was talking about the newspaper, wondering what it would look like. Mrs Perkins came into the classroom looking very pale and serious.

'There's been a problem with the newspaper,' she said, sitting on the edge of her desk. 'For some reason the printers have handed it over to the police.'

I looked at Holly and she stared at me. OH NO! Everyone started mumbling about what it might be. 'I don't know why yet, but I'll let you know as soon as I hear anything,' said Mrs Perkins.

I tried to carry on with the morning lesson about division but I couldn't concentrate - I found it impossible to do a single sum.

Then just before morning playtime Mrs Rizla came into the room. 'Could Holly, Maggie, Sarah and Mandy come to the office, please?' she said.

Everyone watched as we got up and shuffled out. My legs felt like jelly as Mrs Rizla took us into the school office. There in the office were Mum, Holly's dad and two policemen. They wanted to know what we knew about the body in the garden so we had to tell them all about overhearing Mrs Foley.

I was sooooo worried that we'd be in trouble, but the policemen seemed quite friendly. 'We've questioned Mrs Foley,' said the policeman, 'and she says it was a pet goldfish she'd buried. However, we are continuing our investigations.'

A pet goldfish???? Oh dear!

'We realise it was a probably just a foolish mistake,' said the other policemen, 'and no further action will be taken against you, but you really shouldn't be publishing allegations about people, especially if there's no evidence.'

We nodded weakly. I felt awful, like my stomach was full of stones. We walked back to the classroom really slowly, unable to speak.

When we got back, everyone rushed over to us to find out what had happened. We explained the basics of the misunderstanding.

I was in trouble with Mum when I got home. 'Why didn't you tell an adult about what you'd heard?' she asked.

'I don't know,' I said, looking down. 'We wanted it to be an exclusive story for the paper. Please don't tell Dad,' I whispered. She agreed.

Thursday, 6th November

Mrs Foley was off today... Oh no!

There was a big box on Mrs Perkins' desk. 'Well, the newspapers are finally here,' she said. 'The story that the police were interested in has now been removed.'

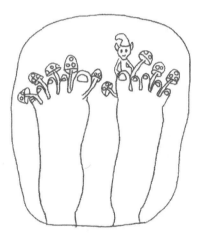

She passed out the papers, dropping one on each desk. As mine landed I noticed that half of the front page was now about our new world record, complete with the brilliant photo, and the other half of the page just had a strange drawing with no story. I looked closely at it, trying to work out what it was. It looked like toes covered in mushrooms. I looked at Holly. 'I don't know how that got in there,' she said.

People were waving the papers around and talking about the toes, wondering what it was all about. At lunchtime we saw Mr Blott rushing around not looking at anyone.

After lunch we went into the playground and saw a big crowd around the picnic table. We squeezed through to see what was going on. Shockingly, there were eight people crammed under the table. Looks like the world record has been smashed already!

Friday, 7th November

Mandy, Holly, Sarah and I tried to hide behind the people in front during assembly today. We bent forward, hoping Mrs Foley wouldn't see us.

'Good afternoon, everybody,' she said. 'I'm sure you've all heard the story about the body in the garden by now,' she continued, as we crouched down a little lower. 'Well, I can assure you it was just my pet goldfish who died from natural causes, so I don't want to hear any more about it.'

We then listened to Year One singing a song about the life cycle of a frog. Every time they sang the word 'frog', Mandy pointed at me (thanks Mandy). After that Mrs Foley stood up again. 'Don't forget,' she said, 'that my garden is part of the Best Autumn Garden competition. It will be on the show on Saturday so please consider voting.'

'I can't believe we're not in more trouble,' said Holly at the end of the day.

'I know. I thought we'd get a hundred detentions,' I said.

'I thought we'd all go to prison when I saw those policemen,' chimed in Sarah.

Saturday, 8th November
BEST AUTUMN GARDEN COMPETITION – THE LIVE SHOW

Rain, rain, rain.

It rained for most of today so we did lots of inside things. I helped Dad make a goat-shaped tool rack for his shed (don't ask). Then we watched TV and had a game of Scrabble. Joppin kept cheating by hiding all the As and Es up his sleeve, which made it very difficult for everyone else. After tea the rain stopped briefly so we went into the garden and played on the wet tyre. I tried not to look at the toilet seat chairs, which were covered in drips.

I managed to swing upside down on the tyre, which was quite good until Joppin spun me round until I felt sick. I was just recovering when I heard Mum calling me, 'Maggie, *Best Autumn Garden* is starting.' We raced in, keen to see Mrs Foley's garden, and leapt onto the sofa as the music began. Suddenly, there was a shot of Mrs Foley's house, which I recognised from when we'd looked over the wall.

'Sadly,' said the voiceover, 'the garden that belongs to this house is not looking as good as usual.' We looked at each other, wondering why. Then it cut to a shot of the garden. It was like a huge puddle with piles of mud and a digger parked in one corner. An upside-down dog sculpture could just be seen under the water. No plants were visible at all. 'This garden,' the voiceover continued, 'has been part of a police investigation, but don't worry, nothing unusual was found. I'm afraid it's unlikely to win this year's competition though, but feel free to vote if you like messy, disgusting places.' A phone number then came up on the screen.

Mum and I looked at each other and my heart started thumping loudly. Joppin ran off to get a pen and wrote the number on his hand. Then they showed the rest of the gardens, which were all beautiful and full of amazing plants.

'Oh dear,' I muttered.

'I wonder if they found the goldfish?' Dad asked.

This was particularly concerning as Mum had said she wouldn't tell Dad about it.

Joppin got the phone. 'Shall we vote for Mrs Foley?'

'I think we'd better,' said Mum.

Monday, 10th November

Everyone was talking about Mrs Foley's garden today. Quentin shook his head slowly as he walked past us. There was even a special morning assembly about it.

'Thank you,' said Mrs Foley once we were all sitting neatly in our assembly rows, with the four of us keeping our heads down. 'Thank you to all those who voted for my garden,' she said. 'Surprisingly, I got 7,000 votes.' Everyone started clapping. 'However,' she continued, 'I was still in last place.' Holly, Mandy, Sarah and I glanced at each other.

'But,' said Mrs Foley, raising her arms in the air, 'I will carry on. I will get my garden back and I will enter next year. The most important thing in life is to use obstacles as stepping stones to success.'

After assembly we had creative writing. We had to write a story about overcoming an obstacle. I wrote about an ant that was trying to complete the world's biggest obstacle course. It was actually quite funny, especially the bit where it took him sixteen years to get through the scramble net.

'Would anyone like to share his or her story?' asked Mrs Perkins towards the end of the lesson. Quentin's hand shot up.

'Go on, Quentin.'

Quentin read out his story. It was all about obstacles to industrial growth in Europe. It was extremely boring and not really a story. I decided not to read mine out.

Wednesday, 12th November

I didn't sleep well last night. I kept thinking about the whole Mrs Foley thing. I know it was a misunderstanding but her garden was ruined because of us. I wanted to say sorry but I couldn't quite face going up to her, so I wrote a small note to put on the staffroom door. It said, 'I'm sorry about your garden'.

After school today Joppin lay on the sofa with the orange blanket over his head and refused to speak to anyone. Eventually, Mum came in to see him. I pretended to leave the room but I hid behind the door so I could listen.

'Come on, Joppin, you can talk to me. I won't tell anyone,' she said.

'Well,' said a little voice from under the blanket, 'when I was outside school waiting for you, a big boy pushed me.'

'Who was it?' asked Mum.

'I don't know. I think he was from another school.'

'Okay,' she said, rubbing his head through the blanket then leaving the room. I went back and sat next to him.

Even though Joppin's often very annoying, I hate to see him upset.

'I'll wait with you tomorrow,' I said. 'Hey, let's watch *The Invisible Boy*.' I turned on the TV. *The Invisible Boy* is Joppin's favourite TV show so I knew he'd come out from under the blanket. It worked and we watched it together, even though I don't really like it and would much rather have watched *Bedroom Makeover* or *Challenge of the Day*.

Thursday, 13th November

I waited with Joppin after school – no sign of the bully, phew!

Friday, 14th November

Still no sign of the bully.

Saturday, 15th November

'Are you still making and selling pompoms?' asked Mum at breakfast.

'Oh yes.' I'd forgotten about my pompom business.

'Well, I need sixteen,' said Mum.

'What for?'

'It's a surprise.'

I spent the rest of the day making pompoms. Each one takes quite a long time and my fingers were aching by the end. I managed to complete ten today.

Sunday, 16th November

I made six more pompoms today and Mum bought all of them, giving me a total of £16. Whooooopeeeedooooo!

HOLIDAY FUND = £22

I kept asking Mum what they were for but she said she couldn't tell me yet. Mysterious!

At teatime we all sat with our fish and peas.

'Come on, eat up your peas, Joppin,' said Mum.

'I can't. They remind me of the bully,' he said, pushing them to one side.

'How can peas remind you of the bully?' asked Mum.

'Green hat,' replied Joppin.

Monday, 17th November

Today in art we were doing more work about our souvenirs.

'I want you to divide your page into four and draw your souvenir from the front, the back, and then from each side.'

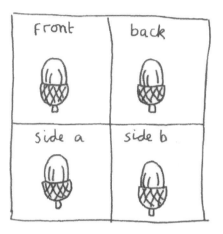

I got my acorn out of my drawer and looked at it from each angle. It looked exactly the same from each view so I started sketching four identical drawings. After about four minutes I'd finished so I drew detailed faces on my two plain rubbers.

After that I looked around to see what everyone else was doing.

Holly's picture of the donkey was quite good although the rear view was a little disturbing, and Sarah's duck was looking very realistic. I glanced at Quentin, who was drawing his mum playing the bagpipes. Because she wasn't there I guess he was drawing from memory. His mum looked much wider than in real life, and in the drawing of the rear she looked enormous. I tried not to giggle.

Tuesday, 18th November

As soon as we went into the classroom we noticed that the drawings we'd done yesterday were on the wall. Quentin's were right in the middle and everyone was looking at the pictures of his mum. Luckily, my acorn pictures were hidden away in a corner, partly covered by Sarah's duck. Everyone had a good laugh at the pictures, especially Quentin's. He got very cross and said we were disrespecting his mother.

Friday, 21st November

OH DEAR!

At the start of school today Quentin's mum bustled into the classroom, elbowing children out of the way. She rushed over to the wall with the drawings on and stared at the picture of her from behind.

'So, is this what Mrs Perkins made you draw?' she asked.

Quentin nodded. 'She said I had to.'

Mrs Perkins came into the classroom and went straight up to Quentin's mum. 'Is everything alright?'

'No, it is not,' said Quentin's mum, pointing at

the picture.

'Oh, it was just an art project,' said Mrs Perkins.

'It is disgraceful and disrespectful. Remove it or I shall complain,' she said, her voice getting quite loud. Then she marched out.

Everyone was very quiet as Mrs Perkins silently removed Quentin's picture and put it in the store cupboard.

Saturday, 22nd November

Well, I found out today what Mum needed the sixteen pompoms for.

'I've got a present for you, Joppin,' she announced this morning. Joppin leapt up and started doing this pigeon dance he does when he's very excited. Mum rushed out then came back with a bag.

Joppin opened it and pulled out the strangest garment I've ever soon. It was like a jumper but it was very lumpy. Joppin held it up, his smile quickly vanishing. He tapped one of the lumps and a pompom fell out and rolled under the sofa.

'What is it?' asked Joppin.

'It's a protection jumper,' said Mum. 'If anyone tries to push you or hurt you, the padded jumper will protect you. Clever, isn't it?'

Joppin just stared at the jumper and silence filled the whole room. Then Dad came in, 'come on, Joppin,' he said, 'try it on.'

'If I wear this, I'm much more likely to get pushed or punched,' said Joppin.

'Exactly, so you'll need the padding for protection,' said Mum.

Joppin reluctantly tried on the jumper, mumbling that he would never wear it in public. 'Don't forget the matching hat,' said Mum, producing a woolly hat full of pompoms from her pocket.

I felt a bit bad for Joppin but at least I got my £16.

Sunday, 23rd November

I saw the protection jumper stuffed down the back of the sofa today. I considered taking all the pompoms out to resell, but I figured I'd better leave it for a while just in case Mum tried to make Joppin wear it again.

We were just about to watch *The Invisible Boy* when Mum ran in.

'Guess what?' She was doing some strange karate chop hand movements.

'What?'

'I've signed you up for judo classes.' We both looked up. 'It's very important that you learn how to defend yourself against bullies,' she added, doing one last karate chop.

'Sounds quite good,' said Joppin, nodding. He turned to me. 'Can I practise on you?' he asked, before leaping on me and pinning me to the sofa. It was a little embarrassing because even though he's smaller than me with extremely thin arms, he managed to pin me down quite easily.

'Maggie, I've signed you up too.'

'Okay, I'll give it a try,' I said. I wasn't completely sure about it, but I didn't want Joppin being trained to the point where he could easily throw me around or pin me down at any time without being able to do anything back.

'Good, because I've rung Sensei Yatsu Yoshi and he's expecting you to start next Saturday.'

For the rest of the day Joppin kept doing very slow forward rolls. 'They're real judo rolls,' he said, but I don't think they were.

Monday, 24th November
JOPPIN'S JUDO SUIT

When we got back from school, there was a judo suit laid out on the floor. 'Wow!' said Joppin, trying it on straight away. It fitted him perfectly and it came with a white belt, which he tied around his waist.

'Oh, you found your suit, Joppin,' said Mum, after she'd put the shopping away. Joppin proceeded to do slow forward rolls in his suit for at least an hour.

'Do I get a suit?' I asked as we were eating tea.

'Yes. I couldn't find one in the second-hand shop though, so I'm making you one.'

This is a bit of a worry. Whenever Mum makes something, it turns out a bit strange. I'll just have to hope it looks like a proper judo suit or I'm going to be mega embarrassed on Saturday.

Friday, 28th November

Nooooooooooooooooooooooooooooooooo!

When I got home today, I saw it straight away. All the blood drained from my head and my fingers went all cold. On a hanger on my bedroom door handle was a very worrying sight. It was kind of the shape of a judo suit but it was made from old white TOWELS!

I rushed downstairs hoping Mum would say it was a joke and whip my real judo suit out of a bag.

'Um, Mum, where's my real judo suit?' I asked.

'Oh, you found it. You'll never believe this but I made it myself from old towels.'

I waited a moment, scanning her face for a giveaway smile that would let me know it was all a terrible joke... but no, she remained serious.

'I can't wear that, it doesn't look right.'

'Maggie, it's fine. I got a judo suit design off the Internet so it's the right shape. It's only the material that's a bit different. And once you've rolled around on the judo mat a few times all the fluffy bits will flatten and it'll look like everyone else's.'

OH NO! I am not looking forward to the judo class tomorrow.

Saturday, 29th November
JUDO DAY

I put on my towel judo suit, much to Joppin's amusement. He kept putting his hands under the tap then chasing me, saying he needed something to dry them on.

I sheepishly got into the car and off we went to Yoshi's Judo Hall. When we got to the car park, we saw lots of kids running into the hall. They were all in proper judo suits. I hid in the car.

'Come on, Maggie, you can't even tell it's made of towels,' said Dad. 'It looks exactly the same as everyone else's.' I looked down, not convinced, but I figured that if I kept moving, perhaps no one would be able to look at the fabric long enough to notice its towellish texture. I got out of the car and started bobbing about.

'It's good to be different anyway. See you in an hour,' said Dad, and he drove off. Everyone had run ahead and was already inside so I made my way towards the door.

I went through a reception hall where there were some toilets and a little café. Luckily, there was no one about. I then saw a door with the words JUDO HALL written on it. I peeped round and saw all the children, including Joppin, kneeling in a row along one side of a huge mat and a big man wearing a black judo suit standing opposite them.

As I opened the door a little wider a loud bell suddenly rang and everyone looked round to see who was coming in. I slid through the door and stood by the mat, wondering if I should join the line and kneel down. The man stared at me. 'Yes?' he asked.

'I'm Maggie. I'm here for the judo class,' I said in a surprisingly high voice.

The man looked at my outfit. 'Well, change out of your dressing gown and into your judo suit quickly.'

I froze, horrified that he thought my judo suit was a dressing gown.

'Okay,' I squeaked, before running out of the hall and into the toilets. I sat on the toilet for an hour until it was time for Dad to collect us. It's quite hard to fill an hour in a toilet cubicle, so I spent quite a lot of time rubbing the towel to make it look more like normal material. (It didn't work.)

'Well, how was it?' asked Mum when we got back.

'Oh, good,' I said. Joppin started giggling.

'I've learnt how to do a real judo roll,' said Joppin, doing a very slow forward roll.

'Oh, Mum, the teacher said I need a proper judo suit,' I said.

'Oh no, I was worried about that. Looks like I'll have to shave it before next week.'

SHAVE IT????? EEEEEEK!

Sunday, 30th November

I was woken up very early by the loud hum of the vacuum cleaner. I opened one bleary eye and looked at the alarm clock... 6.30 a.m. This was very strange because Mum and Dad never get up before nine on a Sunday and they hardly ever vacuum.

Unable to get back to sleep I put on my purple dressing gown and staggered out into the hall. There was Dad, fully dressed and cleaning away. 'Hi, darling,' he said, turning off the vacuum cleaner.

'Um, what's going on?'

'Well, Grandma Merle rang last night. Her flat is about to be decorated so she's moving in here for a month.'

'Really?' I looked around the house. It was very cluttered and I know how very tidy Grandma Merle is. 'When does she get here?'

'Tomorrow night.'

I quickly got dressed. I knew there'd be a lot of work to do and that Joppin and I would be called upon to help.

We had an emergency meeting over breakfast and were all given jobs to do. I had to bag up all the old clothes that Mum had strewn about ready to sell in her eBay shop. (They'll be put in the garage for the four weeks that Grandma Merle is here.) Joppin was to dust everywhere with wet paper towels. Mum was on clutter clearing (i.e. putting most things in the garage) and Dad was on garden tidying.

'Oh no, the toilet seat garden chairs!' said Dad, putting his head in his hands.

'We'll have to hide them,' said Mum. 'You know what she's like about toilet seats. She says they are disgusting.' Mum then told us the story about how when she was little, Grandma Merle used to put a large towel over the toilet between uses so that no one would see it.

All day we bagged, scrubbed, sorted and cleaned. Dad took the legs off the toilet seat stools, and as there was no room left in the garage, he hid them under my bed – gross!!!

After tea we all collapsed, exhausted. The house looked so much better, almost like a normal person's house. As a special reward for all our hard work Mum made some popcorn and we watched a film about a boy who keeps a tiny ghost in his sock drawer... quite good.

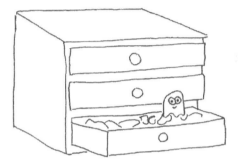

Monday, 1st December
CHRISTMAS PLAY ALERT

'We need to start thinking about this year's Christmas play,' said Mrs Perkins this morning.

'Can I be a huge rabbit?' asked Peter. Everyone laughed.

'Well,' said Mrs Perkins, walking up to him, 'this year anything is possible because we're going to be writing our own play and each of you will come up with a character to be in it.'

Immediately, a wave of excited mumbling swept through the class. This was excellent news!! I usually get the very worst part in the Christmas play. Once I was a camel's post, and one year I was just a tuft of grass! But this year I can choose a character that's funny, has loads of lines, and perhaps does some magic tricks. Oh, the possibilities are endless!

'So,' said Mrs Perkins, 'your homework is to come up with a character. We need the character's name, age, description, job or interests, and think about what makes him or her tick. Have your ideas ready to share on Wednesday, please.' She picked up her whiteboard pen. 'Oh,' she continued, 'regarding the play, there'll be a little twist, but I'll let you know about that later.'

Whoooooooooohoooooooooo!

I was so excited about making up a character that I forgot all about Grandma Merle.

'Shoes on the shoe rack, please,' said Mum as I got home. This was strange, as we didn't have a shoe rack. I looked around the hall then a saw it, a brand new shoe rack tucked under the coat hooks. The shoe pile that usually lives in the corner was gone – all the shoes were now neatly lined up. I put my shoes on the rack and went through to the lounge.

'Maggie!' said Grandma Merle, rushing over to give me a hug. Grandma asked me all about school and I told her about the school play and how we could decide who we wanted to be. 'How marvellous!' she said, clapping her hands. 'What an opportunity to come up with a truly intelligent character!' She agreed to help me with ideas.

Grandma Merle is very keen on education, and after tea she insisted that Joppin and I sat with her while she read bits out of this huge old encyclopaedia. It was all about the construction of bridges.

<u>**Tuesday, 2nd December**</u>

THE SCHOOL PHOTOS HAVE ARRIVED

'Look at you!' squealed Holly, holding the class photo. I had a look, and there, sitting much further back than everyone else and looking tiny and green, was me.

I looked ridiculous and everyone was sniggering and talking about it. I was a bit embarrassed but I did look funny so I giggled about it too. I remembered something Dad said to me once. He said that if people are laughing at you, just laugh along with them then they're not laughing at you any more, everyone's just having a laugh.

Quite useful advice.

'Have you thought of a character yet?' asked Holly at playtime.

'No. Grandma's helping me with it tonight. How about you?'

'I thought,' said Quentin pointing at me 'that you would be Mrs Pea.'

'Very funny,' I said.

'I'm going to be a detective,' said Holly, 'a real one with a magnifying glass on a string around my neck.'

'I'm thinking of being a country and western singer,' said Mandy, 'then I can wear my cowboy boots and do some line dancing.'

We all talked about our ideas for the rest of playtime. Quentin wants to be sixteenth century explorer.

When I got home, I showed Mum and Grandma the class photo. Mum nearly spat her mouthful of tea out when she saw me in it. She had to rush out of the room and I heard snorting and chortling coming from the kitchen. Thanks, Mum!

'What's this green mark?' asked Grandma Merle as she rubbed the photo. 'Is it a mushy pea stain?' I quickly grabbed the picture and took it up to my room to hide it.

After tea I sat down with Grandma Merle to talk about ideas for the play. Grandma was a university professor for 30 years so she knows loads about everything.

'Let's make a general ideas column first,' she said, before writing down loads of ideas on a piece of paper. (Most of her ideas were women from history.) After two hours we decided on who I would be. It was Grandma's idea but I sort of like it. It's a woman scientist called Maria Mitchell. She was an astronomer in the 1800s. I'd rather have been a witch but I didn't want to let Grandma down so Maria Mitchell it is. Apparently, while looking through her telescope in 1843, Maria Mitchell discovered a comet.

I wonder if I'll be able to have a telescope on a string around my neck?

Wednesday, 3rd December

We had to talk about our characters for the play today and were put into groups of six to discuss our ideas. Each group of six will be performing their own mini play in the show. I was in a group with my friends plus Quentin (show-off) and Jake (silly). In our groups we had to talk about how our characters could interact to make a story.

We decided that the explorer could be flying on a comet, Maria Mitchell could see him out of her telescope and a line dancer, a detective and a calculator could enter the room while doing a funny dance. Quentin was not too pleased as he didn't think an explorer would be on a comet, but he was overruled.

Jake's character was a toilet (surprise, surprise). Sarah said that the toilet should just sit quietly on the edge of the stage and the joke would be that everyone would have a turn at sitting on it, Jake thought this was a brilliant idea.

Mrs Perkins said that we'd start working on the dialogue on Friday. I've decided that my character will say a couple of interesting facts about astronomy and physics. Grandma Merle is going to be coming to watch the play and she'll be very impressed by that.

After school Mum asked us to do a judo demonstration for Grandma. She gave me my towelling judo suit, which looked terrible. She'd obviously tried to shave it, but it had only made it look worse, and there were now quite a few holes in it.

We both did slow forward rolls (I had to copy Joppin as I'd missed the lesson) then Joppin pinned me down for ages. 'I like it,' said Grandma, 'but, Maggie, your suit looks awful. I'm going to get you a new one.'

YIPPEE!!

I also found out today that Joppin's class is doing a maths rap in the Christmas concert and he's going to be Pythagoras (some clever maths genius from years ago). Grandma Merle is very impressed.

Friday, 5th December

I got home today to find a brand new judo suit hanging on my door. YIPPEE! It's really nice with thick crisp cotton. I'm sort of looking forward to judo tomorrow now.

Saturday, 6th December
FIRST PROPER JUDO LESSON

I felt much better going to judo in a proper suit. We started with warm-up games then did this really hard exercise. We had to stand with our arms out to our sides for as long as possible. It was mega difficult and my arms were really aching. I only managed two minutes but Joppin could do it for ages and was, in fact, the winner.

After that we had to stand facing a partner then, holding onto their jacket, we had to try and trip them up with our foot. I was quite good because Joppin was my partner and he's much smaller than me, so it was quite easy to knock him off balance.

Sunday, 7th December

Grandma Merle took us to a local pub for Sunday lunch – YUM!

'I'm so proud of you and Joppin,' she said as she tucked into her roast potatoes. 'You're so intelligent. Fancy being Maria Mitchell and Pythagoras in the play. It's wonderful.

Monday, 8th December

OH NO!

I now have a MASSIVE PROBLEM. Eeeeeeeeeek!

We got into our groups for writing the play and I was just sorting out my pencil collection into size order when Mrs Perkins wrote 'THE TWIST' on the whiteboard in big red letters.

'It's very important to be flexible in life,' she said, 'to learn to work with other people creatively and fuse your ideas with theirs.' She sat on her desk and smiled. 'So I've introduced the twist.'

'I can do the twist,' said Jake as he stood up and did a strange dance.

'Not that sort of twist,' continued Mrs Perkins, gesturing at him to sit down. 'You have each created a character for the play. Now you will swap characters with someone else in your group.'

'What? So I can't be a toilet?' asked Jake.

'No, you will be another character and someone else will be the toilet,' said Mrs Perkins.

'That's so unfair, I don't want to be a boring character,' Jake said.

My head went fuzzy as I thought of Grandma - I couldn't swap characters!! She wouldn't be very proud of a line-dancing granddaughter. In a panic I decided to try and be Sarah's calculator then at least I could say a few maths facts.

'Maggie, could you take the register to the office, please?'

Oh no, why me???? I leapt up in a shocked daze and ran to the office as quickly as I could. When I got back, everyone in my group had swapped characters... well, everyone except Jake. The horror is that I am going to be the... TOILET!!!! And Jake is going to be Maria Mitchell. Nooooooooooooooo!! I was too horrified to speak for a while. Jake was sulking in a corner saying it wasn't fair.

We had to work on the script. Because the toilet doesn't say anything I didn't get to suggest many ideas.

I'm very worried about what Grandma will think when she comes to watch the play. I can't tell Mum, Dad or Grandma about my being a toilet as it's just too embarrassing.

Wednesday, 10th December

I still can't tell my family about the toilet thing. I don't know why but I just can't say it and I'm now dreading doing the play.

We were working on costumes today. Yes, my costume involves me sitting on a chair with a toilet seat on my knee. The lid is up and it digs into my face. Jake came in with a telescope swinging around his neck. He's changed the character's name to Matt Mitchell, which I don't think Grandma Merle will like. He keeps making jokes about looking through the telescope and being surprised that things look bigger, which is what I wanted to do.

I had quite a good judo lesson today. We did this exercise where you have to stand against the wall with your legs bent for as long as possible. It's actually really hard to do.

After lunch we put our spindly artificial Christmas tree up.

'You really should get a proper tree,' said Grandma Merle as she rubbed her fingers along a sparse branch.

'It's our traditional tree and we love it, don't we kids?' said Mum. I had to say yes even though I would secretly prefer a proper tree.

Even though we have the spindliest tree in the world, I always like it when it goes up as it makes everything seem so exciting and Christmassy.

Life isn't all good though as I'm still worried about the play, especially as Grandma Merle keeps telling me more facts about Maria Mitchell.

Monday, 15th December

We practised the play today. I felt myself go red every time someone sat on me. I still can't tell my family and I now officially have...

EXTREME TOILET WORRY.

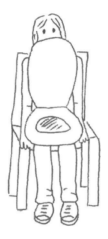

Tuesday, 16th December

The play is going to be on Friday night. This means there are only...

THREE DAYS TO GO UNTIL THE PERFORMANCE.

Mum, Dad, Grandma Merle and Dad's friend Jim-Bob are all going to be there.

TOILET WORRY!

Wednesday, 17th December
We had a full dress rehearsal today.

'You're really good at being a toilet,' said Holly as I helped her finish off her calculator costume.

I still have...

TOILET WORRY.

'I can't wait to see my clever grandchildren on Friday,' said Grandma after tea. 'Maria Mitchell would be so proud if she was still alive.'

Noooooooo!

Thursday, 18th December
ONE DAY TO GO UNTIL THE PERFORMANCE.
TOILET WORRY.

Friday, 19th December
THE PERFORMANCE HAS TAKEN PLACE!!!!!

Well, I was sat on five times. I could hear laughter coming from the audience each time, but I didn't look up so I don't know what Grandma Merle thought of it all.

'I didn't know you were going to be a toilet,' said Mum as we got in the car.

'No, we all had to swap characters,' I said.

'Well, it was really funny. You were a great toilet,' said Mum.

'Was I good?' asked Joppin.

'You were marvellous,' said Grandma Merle, giving him a hug. She didn't look at me.

When we got home, I ran up to my room and lay down for a while. There was a knock at the door.

'Come in,' I called. Grandma Merle opened the door and came and sat on the bed next to me.

'I don't mind that you didn't want to be Maria Mitchell. I'm more upset that you couldn't tell me you wanted to be a toilet.'

'I didn't want to be, the teacher made me swap, that's why I was a toilet,' I said quietly, lying face down on my bed.

'It's fine. If you have an interest in toilets that's great.' I could see her flinch as she said the word 'toilet'.

'But I hate toilets. I have no interest in them at all.'

Just then Grandma Merle's shoe banged on something under the bed. She leaned down to see what it was then pulled out four toilet seats.

We stared at them in silence for quite a long time then Grandma quietly got up and left the room.

Sunday, 21st December

Grandma Merle seems to be okay with me now. She even took Joppin and me to the museum today, phew! No one has mentioned anything about toilets since.

Wednesday, 24th December
JOPPIN'S BIRTHDAY

The Christmas tree was taken down for the day and hidden under the stairs as it's Joppin's birthday. Mum says it's not fair if Joppin's big day is overshadowed by Christmas.

I gave him a book about how to draw cartoon characters, Grandma gave him a maths set, and then Mum and Dad bundled a full bin bag into the room. 'Happy birthday, Joppin,' they said in unison as they handed it to him.

He tore open the bag and the strangest thing I've ever seen fell out. It was a sort of homemade life-size body. It seemed to be a pair of tights, a long-sleeved top and a large sock (the head) sewn together and stuffed. Joppin stared at it for a moment then ran out of the room screaming.

'It's okay, darling,' said Mum, running after him. 'It's just a judo practice dummy that Dad made, and there's one more present.'

Joppin nervously came back in. Dad handed him another plastic bag. He opened it and pulled out my old towel judo suit.

I helped Joppin put the judo suit on the scary dummy then Dad held it up under the arms while Joppin tried to do judo throws on it.

It didn't work that well and it looked terrible, but Joppin's going to have to have it in his room. I'm SOOOOO glad that I haven't got anything like that cluttering up my room.

Thursday, 25th December
MERRY CHRISTMAS!

Mum put the Christmas tree back up last night and even put fairy lights all around the fireplace. It felt really Christmassy when we got up. We sat around the fire in the lounge to open our presents. I gave Grandma a book of puzzles, which she loved. I gave Mum and Dad homemade biscuits, and I gave Joppin a drawing pad and pens to practise drawing his cartoons.

When I opened my present from Mum and Dad, I was rather horrified to find out it was another handmade judo practice dummy. It was even scarier than Joppin's one yesterday as its head was made from a purple sock and it was wearing Dad's old pyjamas. (The pair with the yellow stains - eeeeeek!)

'The pyjamas are a bonus present,' said Mum smiling.

'Thanks, Mum and Dad,' I stammered as I put it to one side and tried not to look at it.

'We didn't want you to be jealous because Joppin had one,' said Dad, squeezing Mum's hand.

Joppin gave me an electric pencil sharpener (quite good) and Grandma Merle gave me a book called *The History of the Toilet*. Hmmmmmmmm.

Overall it was an interesting collection of presents. The pencil sharpener is very good, although all my pencils are now very small due to over-sharpening.

Monday, 29th December

Grandma Merle went home today so Mum and Dad spent the whole day getting all of the junk out of the garage and spreading it around the house. Dad even got the toilet seats out from under my bed and re-made the garden stools.

Monday, 5th January

Exciting news! Somebody small, furry and called Fred has joined our class. Yes, we now have a class hamster!!! Mrs Perkins brought him in this morning and his cage sits in the reading corner. We all crowded round as soon as we saw it but Fred was nowhere to be seen. Eventually he popped his head out of a little wooden house in the cage and then vanished again. Even though I only saw him for a few seconds I can confirm that he is extremely cute with a little twitching nose.

There was a sheet of paper on the wall next to the cage that said 'Weekend Hamster Rota'. This means that it's possible to take Fred home for a weekend. All the dates for January and February had already been taken by the time I got there. I'm going to have to be quicker when the March/April dates go up. I noticed that Holly had claimed the 14th/15th February, so I asked if I could go to her house to help and she said yes!

At playtime we all huddled together to try and stay warm and talked about our Christmas presents. I was amazed at how good everyone else's presents sounded. Sarah got a robot that you control using a computer, Holly got a fashion design kit, and Mandy got £300, shopping vouchers, a gold necklace, theatre tickets, and a chocolate-coin-making machine.

'What did you get?' asked Mandy, turning to me. I was silent for a moment while I tried to work out what to say. I didn't want to mention the toilet book, and the other presents were rather embarrassing, so I decided to tell them about the present Joppin got me.

'Um, an electric pencil sharpener,' I said.

'What else?' asked Mandy.

Hmmmm. I had to think of something else but I couldn't say the judo practice dummy, as it was so awful. 'Oh, a clothes dummy,' I said quietly, hoping that they wouldn't quite hear.

'Wow, like the life-size mannequins that they put clothes on in shops?' asked Sarah.

'That is so brilliant,' said Mandy. 'I would love a shop dummy. You are soooooo lucky.'

'Epic!' said Holly.

I felt my cheeks heating up as I pictured the horrible floppy purple-faced dummy, which was lying under my bed wearing stained pyjamas.

Wednesday, 7th January

'I'm afraid that because of the issues last term we're not going to be able to do a school newspaper this term,' said Mrs Perkins today. Everyone moaned, and I looked down. 'But,' she went on, 'you can make a puzzle book instead.'

We spent the next hour making up word searches and crosswords.

'I can't believe you ruined our chances of making more newspapers,' said Quentin at playtime. He looked very annoyed, as did some of the other kids too. Oh dear.

Friday, 9th January

We noticed that the hamster was awake when we went into the classroom this morning. This is quite rare because he seems to be asleep in his little wooden house nearly all the time. Mrs Perkins says it's because he's nocturnal so he's mainly active in the evening and during the night. Sarah, who has her own hamster at home, is mega confident with animals and she opened the cage to get him out. She passed him to me and I felt his soft warmth on my hand. I could feel his little heart beating so fast as I stroked his head and looked into his black eyes.

Mrs Perkins came in so I popped him back in the cage and went to my desk. I can't wait until I get a chance to take him home, it is going to be brilliant. I've already started collecting toilet roll tubes so I can make little tunnels for him and I'm designing a hamster obstacle course. It'll have tunnels, a bridge, a see-saw and a swing.

It'll be ages until I get a chance to take him home though. He's already booked up until the end of February and the sign-up sheets for March and April aren't even up yet. I'm going to have a lot more toilet roll tubes stored up by the time it's my turn.

Steam poured out of our mouths as we huddled next to the picnic table at playtime. Holly had brought her hand-warmer in and she let me have a go. It was so soft and fluffy and warmed my hands up really quickly. It's made out of a tube of brown fake fur, which hangs on a string around the neck. I'm going to ask Mum if she can have a go at making me one.

91

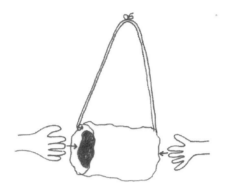

'It's my birthday in three weeks,' said Holly excitedly, 'so I'm planning my party. I've already thought of a theme.'

'Oh, what is it?' I asked, rubbing my hands together inside the hand-warmer.

'You remember I told you I'd got that fashion design kit for Christmas?' we all nodded, 'well it gave me the idea to have a fashion design party.'

'Sounds fab,' said Mandy.

'Yes,' said Holly, 'everyone will design a t-shirt or something then later in the party we'll wear our designs down a catwalk… It'll be like a fashion show.'

'Brilliant!' said Mandy, jumping up and doing a fancy walk.

'My dad,' continued Holly, 'says he can borrow a pop-up catwalk-type structure that will fit in St Margaret's Hall.'

It sounded really good and I had a big smile on my face.

'I can picture it now,' said Holly, 'and Maggie, your clothes dummy can be at the end of the catwalk dressed in some amazing outfit. That will look sooooo good. Can I borrow it?'

My smile wavered. 'Um, of course,' I mumbled, my brain scrambling about for ideas of ways to make sure my dummy never appeared at the party.

Oh dear, I need to come up with a plan.

Saturday, 10th January

I looked at the hideous purple-faced dummy in its stained pyjamas and wondered if I could make it look more like a real mannequin. Could I perhaps put a real doll's head on it or something? The answer was no, as any old dolls that were lying around would have heads that were much too small.

Perhaps I can tell Holly I've lost it or I can say my mum won't allow me to use it. Eeeeeeeeek!

Sunday, 11th January

Today I asked Mum if she would make me a hand-warmer. I described exactly what Holly's one looked like. I even did a sketch and she seemed to get the idea. I'm so excited about having my own hand-warmer. I just wish I didn't have...

DUMMY WORRY.

Monday, 12th January

I had a look on eBay last night to see how much it would cost to buy a proper shop mannequin and the very cheapest one is £67. That's £44 more than I have.

All I can hope for is that Holly forgets about using my dummy altogether.

Wednesday, 14th January

OH NO!!!!

Last night Holly's dad rang my dad and said he'd heard we had a dummy, he then asked if he could borrow it for Holly's party. Dad was delighted and said yes straight away. He even offered to drive it to St Margaret's Hall on the big day.

'Isn't it great that Holly wants to use the dummy for her fashion party?' said Dad at teatime.

'Kind of,' I said, 'but she really needs a dummy that stands up so she might be better getting one somewhere else.'

'Nonsense,' said Dad, 'I think I can build some sort of frame that will make it stand up.'

OH NO!

Thursday, 15th January

SNOW

When I woke up this morning, everything was covered in snow. I looked out of the window and watched the large fluffy flakes slowly tumble down.

Joppin was really excited and immediately went outside to roll around in it.

After breakfast I got dressed and put on my purple wellies and hat. I was just about to look for my gloves when Mum ran in.

'You don't need gloves today,' she said, a big smile creeping over her face, 'because your hand-warmer's ready.'

Hooray, I thought, a hand-warmer at last! I waited excitedly as Mum went to get it. She came back with something very strange. It was a pair of upside-down underpants with some string sewn onto them. I looked at the item in horror. 'What is it?' I asked.

'Clever, isn't it,' said Mum. 'You put your hands in the leg holes and I've sewn up the waist bit. It's a better design than Holly's because the hands go in at a more natural angle.'

I considered running out but I didn't want to hurt Mum's feelings, so I shoved the 'hand-warmer' in my pocket and headed for the door.

'Um, thanks, Mum,' I shouted as I left for school.

In the playground this morning everyone was busy making snowballs and throwing them around. Quentin got me right in the face!!! The cold wet snow was dripping from my eyes and felt awful. I couldn't really make one to throw back because I didn't have time to find my gloves, and when I tried to make one with my bare hands, the snow was too cold.

Holly ran up to me and brushed some of the snow off my face.

'Guess what I've got,' she said, getting some envelopes out of her bag. She looked through them and gave me one. 'Invitations to my party,' she said.

I opened it.

Dear Maggie

You are invited to Holly's fashion party on Saturday, 7th February at St Margaret's Hall. Starts at 3 p.m. and finishes with a fashion show at 7 p.m.

THE EVENT WILL FEATURE MAGGIE'S
FANTASTIC LIFE-SIZE MANNEQUIN.

I gulped when I read the last bit. Oh dear, I wonder if I can make the dummy look better before the party.

Holly rushed around the playground handing out loads of invitations. It seemed like just about everyone was invited, even Quentin.

Saturday, 17th January

It's still snowing and judo was cancelled today because there was so much snow. I just spent the day hanging around watching TV with Joppin.

Sunday, 18th January

Joppin and I were lying on the sofa watching *The Invisible Boy* this morning when Mum came in.

'Could you two shovel the snow off the drive? I'll pay you.'

When we heard that there was money involved, we raced upstairs to get dressed. I needed more money for my holiday fund so it was great news.

We spent four hours outside shovelling away. It was extremely hard work as the snow was deep and compact. At around lunchtime we came in and flopped exhausted onto the sofa.

'You did a good job,' said Mum, looking out of the window, 'here's your money.'

She then gave us five pence each. Five pence!?!?!?! That won't even buy one sweet.

I put it in my moneybox.

HOLIDAY FUND = £22.05

Monday, 19th January

The playground is still full of snow and we got pelted with snowballs again. (Thanks, Quentin!)

Everyone was talking about Holly's party as they stomped around in their wellies.

'It's great that there'll be a real mannequin,' said Claire. 'That will look so cool.'

Holly told everyone that we'll be customising t-shirts and jeans, then, if we want to, we can wear our designs for the catwalk show at the end.

'The best design will go on the mannequin,' she said, linking my arm. I tried to smile as my brain fuzzed in a panic.

Friday, 23rd January

The snow has just about melted now. There's just a bit of slush here and there. I still don't know what to do about the dummy/mannequin problem. Worryingly, Dad has been spending a lot of time in his shed working on the 'frame'.

Saturday, 24th January

Judo was on today. Our warm-up game was dodge ball. We used this sponge ball and it was really fun trying to hit people with it. After that we did a lot of pin-downs. Quite good.

In the afternoon Mum took me to town to look for Holly's birthday present. I got a really nice owl notebook and matching owl pen from Paperchase. I have to be very careful about getting people presents as Mum has a tendency to try and make things if she can get away with it.

Tuesday, 27th January

All the snow has gone now and it's quite a bit warmer. I went into the playground this morning to look for the others.

THWACK!!

Suddenly, a snowball hit me on the back of my head. I felt it slide down the inside of my coat. I swung round in surprise and saw Quentin peeping out from behind a tree. He then threw another snowball at Mandy.

'Where did you get the snow from?' asked Holly. 'It's all melted.'

'Made them last week and kept them in the freezer,' said Quentin, holding up a freezer bag and laughing.

Friday, 30th January

Oh no, only one week and one day to go until the fashion party. The problem is, even if I could get a proper mannequin, Dad would be upset because he's so pleased that the one he made is being used.

Noooooooooooooo!

Saturday, 31st January

After judo today I got the dummy out from under my bed. I had a good long look at it and wondered what to do.

The body is floppy, but perhaps Dad's frame (as yet unseen by anyone but him) will make it stand up and look kind of okay. The stuffed purple sock doesn't look like a proper head at all though, and the yellow buttons that Mum sewed on for eyes make it look seriously weird.

I know! There are some plastic googly eyes in Mum's craft box - perhaps they will look more realistic. I could even use skin-coloured plasters to make eyelids so that the eyes look less googly.

I have an idea about the purple face colour too. Mum has this make-up bag with skin-coloured foundation cream in it. I'll try rubbing some of that on the head.

February

Sunday, 1st February

OH NO!!!!!!!!!

It's less than a week to go until the party and the dummy's now looking worse than ever. The skin-coloured cream didn't rub in properly and the face now looks like it's covered in weird pink stains, the new eyes look scary, and the eyelids (made of plasters) make it look half asleep.

One good thing did happen today though. Holly's actual birthday is next Tuesday and Holly's mum rang my mum to see if I wanted to join Holly for a birthday meal at Belle's restaurant on Tuesday night. This is exciting news because Belle's restaurant is the poshest restaurant in town. YIPPEEEEE!

Monday, 2nd February

Eeeeeeek! Only five days to go until the party. All the girls are talking about it now, saying how much they hope they win the competition so their design can be on the mannequin.

'I wish there was still snow,' moaned Jake at playtime. This has given me the brilliant idea of making some pompom snowballs to sell. I really need to get more money in the holiday fund, as even though I'm doing quite well, I still only have £22.05.

Tuesday, 3rd February
HOLLY'S ACTUAL BIRTHDAY

After school I rushed in to get ready to go to Belle's restaurant. I wore my black leggings, my black top and my best silver sparkly cardigan.

'Don't forget your hand-warmer,' said Mum as I put my coat on. She stuffed the ludicrous underpants hand-warmer into my coat pocket as I ran out and got into Holly's car.

'Wow!' said Holly as we arrived at the restaurant. It looked absolutely amazing. It was dark but the restaurant was all lit up with twinkling golden fairy lights. Even the trees had little lights wrapped around them.

As we walked in a man dressed in a suit took our coats. I handed mine over but was horrified to see the underpants hand-warmer hanging out of my coat pocket as the man carried it off to hang it up somewhere.

'This way to your table,' said a woman in a red dress and very high heels. We all followed her through the busy restaurant, listening to her clip-clopping as she walked. We were given a glass table right at the back and we sat down excitedly.

'Please make sure your children behave properly,' said the woman to Holly's dad as she handed out the menus. She turned to Holly and me, 'and don't you dare make a mess,' she sneered, her eyes narrowing into a nasty stare. She then turned and flounced off, clip-clopping into the distance.

'What a horrible woman!' said Holly's mum, and we all agreed. Luckily, someone else came to take our orders and we soon forgot about her. Holly's dad ordered wine and Holly and I ordered orange juice. We then asked for loads of tapas, which we all agreed we'd share.

Soon after, all these little bowls of different foods like olives, cheeses, fried squid (eeek!) and loads of other bits and bobs arrived. It was really fun sharing everything, I'm not so sure about the squid though.

We'd nearly finished the tapas and I was eyeing up a rather tasty-looking ice cream sundae on a nearby table when loads of people started laughing. We all looked around to see what was going on. More people joined in the laughter. Suddenly, we saw what was causing all the hilarity. The woman in the red dress who'd been rude to us earlier was walking across the restaurant with MY underpants hand-warmer hanging from the back of her dress. It looked SOOOOOOO funny.

'Oh no, her knickers!' said Holly, covering her mouth.

The woman walked past a nearby table. 'Excuse me, Miss,' said a man with a super neat moustache. 'I think something's happened to your underwear.' The woman turned in horror and grabbed the hand-warmer. Her face went as red as her dress. 'They're not mine,' she squeaked, as she rushed off towards the bathroom. Everyone in the restaurant was talking about it. We didn't see the woman again. I think she must have stayed in the bathroom all evening. Oh dear!

Holly and I ordered ice cream sundaes, which came in very tall glasses with extremely long spoons.

So now I'm back in my bedroom after a brilliant evening.

Oh no.......

I've just seen one of the dummy's legs sticking out from under my bed, which has reminded me about...

DUMMY WORRY.

Aaaaaaagh! Only four days to go.

Thursday, 5th February

After school today I made four snowball pompoms. It's the only thing that takes my mind off dummy worry. As long as I'm stuffing wool through a hole in a piece of cardboard I don't really think about it too much. But as soon as I stop my thoughts return to the dummy.

OH NO! Two days to go.

Friday, 6th February

I got in from school and flopped onto the sofa. Suddenly, I heard lots of strange banging noises then I saw Dad coming into the lounge carrying a large wooden square. It was nearly as tall as him and clearly hard to move about. It had a kind of stand as well that got caught on the doorframe. It looked very strange. 'What is it?' I asked as he finally got it into the room and put it down in front of the TV.

'It's the frame for the dummy, ready for the party tomorrow,' he said.

My mouth fell open. 'It can't be,' I said. 'It's too big to go inside the dummy.'

'No, the dummy goes in the frame. Come on, let's try it out.'

I was too shocked to move, so in the end Dad went up to my room and got the dummy. He then spent a while stringing it up in the frame. It made a kind of star shape – its hands and feet tied into the corners. It looked utterly ridiculous. Joppin came in and burst out laughing. He was laughing so much that he couldn't breathe properly and Dad had to pat him on the back.

'Yes, the frame works well,' he said as he untied the dummy.

OH NO! I'm so dreading tomorrow.

Saturday, 7th February
PARTY NEWS

I'm just back from Holly's party and sleepover. I can't believe all that has happened.

I woke up very early yesterday morning, in fact, I'm not sure I slept at all. As I lay in bed, my mind just kept filling up with terrible images of the dummy. I got out of bed and crept downstairs really quietly. The outside light was on and I could see Dad out of the window. He was attaching the dummy to the frame, which he'd put on the roof of the car. It seemed very early in the day to be getting it ready as the party wasn't until 3 p.m.

I watched him struggle, balanced on a stool trying to tie the hands to the top corners of the frame. Freezing rain, lit up by the outdoor light, surrounded him and I could see he was shaking. Soon my eyes drifted from my dad to the strange dummy. It looked scary, weird and just plain wrong as it hung there, it's purple and pink head flopping down.

I was dreading taking it to the party. I had a plan though. The plan was to take an old duvet cover and put it over the dummy once we arrived, then hide the whole thing somewhere in St Margaret's Hall. If anyone asked where it was, I was going to say I'd lost it.

'Hello, darling,' said Dad, breathing into his hands as he came inside.

'Isn't it a bit early to be putting the dummy on the car?' I asked.

'Ah well, best to be prepared,' he said.

He made me a bowl of cornflakes and I ate it on the sofa. This would never normally be allowed if Mum was up but she and Joppin were still asleep.

Dad got himself a cup of tea then sat on the sofa next to me.

'You know, Maggie,' he said, taking a sip, 'there's nothing better than making something that's actually useful.'

I smiled and wondered where in St Margaret's Hall I'd be able to hide it.

We watched one of my favourite shows about girls turning into mermaids and Dad sang along with the theme tune. I'm sure he watches it while I'm at school.

'Thanks, Dad,' I said, 'for making the frame and everything.'

Dad smiled and I could see a little tear in his eye.

At 2.30 Dad and I set off for the party. I'd suggested we go quite early and I bundled the old duvet cover into the car too.

'I just want the dummy to be a surprise for later,' I told Dad when he asked what the duvet cover was for, 'so we'll cover it up when we arrive.' Luckily, Dad thought it was a good idea.

When we got there, I helped to get the dummy, still in the frame, off the roof as quickly as possible. We then put the duvet cover over it. St Margaret's Hall was open so we carried it in and I hid it in a little side room.

A minute later I saw Holly running around with a huge pile of t-shirts. 'Great, you're here,' she said. 'Can you help?'

I kissed Dad goodbye and went to help carry t-shirts from Holly's dad's car into the hall.

THE PARTY

All the plain t-shirts and jeans were put out on tables around the edges of the room. There was a stage at the front, and coming out of the stage was the catwalk. No one mentioned the mannequin.

Soon everyone arrived and there was great excitement as people sat down and began designing their clothes. There were fabric pens, special glue, buttons, ribbons, and loads of other bits and bobs. We all got to work.

'I love your t-shirt,' said Holly as I sewed on another gold ribbon. Hers was covered in the names of everyone in the class. Quentin, who was opposite us, was drawing a big scary eyeball on his. It actually looked quite good – he'd even sewn on bits of red to be the veins.

After an hour of so all the t-shirts and jeans were put to one side and the tables were cleared and set out with a party tea. It was very good, and there was even a big chocolate fountain in the corner of the room that we dipped bits of fruit into.

A bit later Holly's dad started closing the curtains and setting up some disco lights. I guessed it was ready for the fashion show. I was delighted because it was looking like the dummy had been forgotten.

Lots of people got changed into their new t-shirts or jeans.

'I can't find my t-shirt,' said Quentin.

Suddenly, Mandy screamed and pointed. There was Holly's dad carrying the dummy, still tied up in the frame, out onto the catwalk. It looked very scary indeed and it wore a pair of sequin-covered jeans and Quentin's eyeball t-shirt.

'My goodness, what's that?' asked Holly. I started feeling very strange, kind of numb. Everyone started laughing and pointing at it.

'That's the dummy,' I whispered to Holly and Mandy. Holly covered her face with her hands then started giggling.

'Why is my t-shirt on the monster?' asked Quentin.

'It's a monster!' shouted Jake.

The music began and we all lined up to do our walk down the catwalk. Jake went first and did a monster walk, his legs apart, his arms up, and his head flopping just like the dummy. The people behind him followed. The dummy was at the end of the catwalk and as people walked round it, they looked at it and did a fake scream. It became really funny, and after the show everyone ran up to Holly saying that they loved the monster-themed fashion show and that it was a great idea to have a real monster model on the stage.

'I think the monster was the best bit of the party,' said Claire.

After the fashion show Holly's dad played some music and everyone danced (lots of monster dancing) in their new clothes. He even found a song about a monster. The words were, 'What's that coming over the hill, is it a monster?' He played that one loads of times.

When the party was over, Dad came to pick up the dummy. 'The kids loved that model,' said Holly's dad as he helped Dad put it on the car roof. Dad beamed.

Mandy, Sarah and I went back to Holly's house for the sleepover.

'Your dummy was so funny,' said Sarah.

'It was brilliant,' said Holly, linking my arm.

We gave Holly her presents; she loved the owl notebook and pen.

As I lay in the sleeping bag, once the others were asleep, I smiled. No more dummy worry for me.

Monday, 9th February

Everyone's talking about how good Holly's party was. 'That monster model was amazing,' said Peter.

'Can I borrow it for my party?' asked Jake.

It seems that the horrible dummy was the star of the show. Even Mrs Perkins had heard about it and she asked us all to write about monsters in our creative writing lesson.

Wednesday, 11th February

Even though all the snow has melted and there's been no snow at all for several days, I got hit with a snowball again today. It landed right on the top of my head and made my hair really wet. I saw Quentin running behind a tree with his cooler bag. 'Better watch out,' he sniggered.

It did remind me about my snowball pompoms though and I made a few more tonight. I'm going to bring them into school to try and sell them on Friday.

Friday, 13th February

I took my pompoms into school today, ready to sell.

'Good morning, children,' said Mrs Foley as we all sat in the hall for assembly.

'Good morning, Mrs Foley, good morning, everyone,' we all sang back.

'We have a visitor today. Please welcome Police Inspector Morvel,' she said. A very round-looking policeman walked into the hall. I recognised him straight away as one of the policemen who had come to see us about the newspaper story. I looked at Holly in alarm and we both crouched down. I really hoped it was nothing to do with us.

'Children,' he said, crossing his arms, 'there was an incident outside this school yesterday morning.' I breathed a huge sigh of relief. 'I was walking along the pavement when someone threw a white ball at me. It very nearly hit me on the nose.'

Everyone looked at Quentin, who looked out of the window and did a silent whistle.

'It was,' continued Inspector Morval, 'like a snowball, but as there's no snow, it must have been something else. Unfortunately it landed in a bush and I couldn't retrieve it.'

I caught Quentin's eye and could see a small smile on his face. Mrs Foley stood up.

'Throwing things at people will never be tolerated,' she said. She then gave a looooooong talk about respecting people, especially the police and teachers.

At the end of assembly we all had to walk past Mrs Foley and Inspector Morvel as we left the hall. Just as I was walking past, one of the white pompoms I'd hidden up my jumper fell out and rolled very near the policeman's feet. Mrs Foley and the policeman stared at me. I froze mid-step, completely unable to move.

'Maggie, come and see me at lunchtime,' said Mrs Foley.

I swallowed hard and my body became mine again. I nodded and ran out.

OH NO!!!!!

At lunchtime I knocked very quietly on the door of Mrs Foley's office and she called me in.

'Well, have you got something to tell me?' asked Mrs Foley, gesturing for me to sit down on the green chair opposite her desk.

'Um, it wasn't me,' I said quietly. I promised that I had nothing to do with it. She didn't look convinced but said she'd give me the benefit of the doubt this time.

'But I'll be watching you,' she said as I was leaving the room.

I did manage to sell four pompoms today though, so I now have £26.05 in the holiday fund.

Sunday, 15th February

This weekend Fred, the hamster, has been staying at Holly's house, and today I went round for tea to help look after him. I took three snow pompoms round in case Holly's sisters were interested in buying them. (They weren't – strange.)

We sat in Holly's room and put a strawberry in Fred's cage, hoping the smell would wake him up.

114

Luckily, it worked and the hamster poked his twitchy nose out of his little wooden house. He ran up to the strawberry, put the whole thing in his mouth, then pushed it into his cheek before running off back to his little home. A minute later he came out again and Holly lifted him up really gently. She passed him to me and I looked at his little black shiny eyes. Holly and I then sat on the floor and made a square with our legs for Fred to run about it.

'I've got a brilliant idea,' I said, reaching into my pocket and getting one of the white pompoms out. I handed it to Fred, who immediately took hold of it with his teeth.

'Oh look!' said Holly as Fred ran around carrying it. It looked so cute, like a pompom carrying a pompom.

After tea we sat on Holly's bed taking it in turns to hold and stroke Fred.

'How's the monster doing?' asked Holly.

'Still under the bed,' I said quietly. We both smiled.

'You're so funny,' she said.

'I should have said it wasn't a real mannequin, it was just when I said 'dummy', everyone just assumed...'

'It was better than a real mannequin,' said Holly, passing Fred to me.

115

<u>**Monday, 16th February**</u>

When we went into our classroom today, we saw that '**OLDER PERSON PROJECT**' was written on the whiteboard.

'We're starting an exciting new project,' said Mrs Perkins as she sat on her desk. 'You will each befriend an older person over the next few weeks then you will write about how it went and what you learnt.' She handed out some nice new blue notebooks with the words 'My Older Person Project' printed on the front.

'Can I befriend my sister, she's older?' asked Holly.

'No, you need to befriend a really old person, grandparent age or older,' replied Mrs Perkins.

'Can it be a grandparent?' asked Jake.

'Yes, it can if you see the grandparent regularly enough.'

Hmmmmmm, that meant mine couldn't be Grandma Merle as I hardly ever see her.

Mrs Perkins then said that if anyone was really struggling to find someone, she would get someone from a nearby old people's home.

At playtime we all talked about our older person ideas.

'I might do my neighbour, Miss Fash,' said Holly, 'she's really nice.'

'There's this old woman at my chess club,' said Sarah. 'It'd be good to befriend her because we can play chess and chat at the same time.' Mandy looked at her and yawned.

'Actually, my Mum's friend is a grandma and she's only 38 so I might have her,' said Mandy.

'I'm not sure that's what Mrs Perkins had in mind,' said Holly.

We each took a letter home about the project and how to stay safe. It said that a parent should be there every time we meet up with our older person. Hmmmmm, I'm not sure that Mum's going to like that.

I still don't have a clue who to befriend, there aren't that many older people around here. I'm going to ask Mum for ideas.

Tuesday, 17th February

'My older person is a celebrity,' said Quentin, coming up and sitting on the picnic table at playtime, 'so I'm pretty sure my project will be the best.'

'Who is it?' asked Holly.

'He's called Bruce, but I can't tell you any more.'

I still didn't know who mine would be. Mum's only idea was Ida, who works in the local sewing shop.

117

She's this horrible woman who always tells me off for running my hands through the mixed button trays, so I don't fancy befriending her.

Thursday, 19th February

We all hoped Mrs Perkins had forgotten about the souvenirs but she hadn't, and we had to make clay models of them today. My clay acorn was really bad and it looked like a small lump in a wonky cup.

'Why have you made model of a used potty?' asked Quentin. 'That's gross.' Jake looked over and smiled before doing a thumbs up.

As I was walking home I saw Mr Alimo building a small plastic greenhouse in his front garden. As soon as I saw him I decided that he'd be the perfect person for the project.

'Hello,' I said cheerfully as I walked past. Unfortunately, he ignored me... hmmmmmm.

I'm still keen for Mr Alimo to be my older person as he seems to know all about gardening and I'd quite like to find out about it. I wouldn't mind growing some food one day, perhaps strawberries and raspberries, and possibly the odd bean to give to Mum.

Saturday, 21st February

We had judo today. There's going to be a competition with another club in a month so we did loads of practice matches. It was quite fun, although this big girl called Martha kept pinning me down, which was rather alarming.

After judo I decided to go and see Mr Alimo. I had to take Mum with me in accordance with the letter, so we wandered down the street. Mum was carrying a hand-knitted egg cosy as a gift for him, which was rather embarrassing.

He was inside the small plastic greenhouse laying out some trays. He didn't notice us hanging around so after a while we went home. Mum left the egg cosy on his garden wall.

Monday, 23rd February

'So,' said Mrs Perkins, 'who has found an older person to befriend?' Nearly all the pupils put their hand up, including me.

'Jake, who's yours?' she asked.

'Mine is James McCoy,' he said, tipping back on his chair.

'And where did you meet him?'

'At a graveyard.'

There was a shocked intake of breath around the room.

'Does he work there?' said Mrs Perkins, sounding worried.

'No, he lives there... Well, he doesn't exactly live.'

'Go on,' said Mrs Perkins.

'His name is on one of the graves... but you never said the older person had to be alive.'

Mrs Perkins shook her head in disbelief. 'We'll talk later, Jake.' She looked around the room. 'Maggie, who's yours?'

'Um, mine is a man who lives on my street, he's called Mr Alimo,' I said.

'Sounds great,' she replied.

So that's it. Mr Alimo has to be my older person now as I've told Mrs Perkins about him. Hmmmmm. I'm going to have to find a way to talk to him about it – perhaps I'll pop round tomorrow afternoon.

Saturday, 28th February

We got to judo a bit early today so I hung around by the café looking at the notice board. There was a big poster up that said 'Bell Farm Pet Show' with a sign-up sheet attached to it. I'd never heard of Bell Farm but I figured it must be nearby if the poster's up at the judo hall.

I really wish I had a pet to enter into a pet show. Mum says we can't have one though as it's too much trouble. She even said a goldfish was too much work.

After judo it was pouring with rain. For some reason Mum had parked in the space furthest away from the door and we had to run for it. Joppin and I were soaking wet and freezing by the time we dived into the car and slammed the doors shut. My wet hair was plastered to my face and drips of water ran down my cheeks. I was shivering all the way home. When we got back, I changed straight into my pyjamas even though it was only lunchtime. I decided to wait for better weather before visiting Mr Alimo and I watched TV with Joppin instead. There was a film with a character called Mike who wore a green hat.

'Is he like your bully?' I asked Joppin.

'Oh that, no, he wasn't a bully. He just bumped into me by accident.'

Hmmmmm, sounds like the whole bullying thing may have been exaggerated. Hmmmm, the bullying was the whole reason we ended up doing judo. Well, judo is sort of fun so maybe it wasn't so bad. I ruffled Joppin's damp hair and he hid under the orange blanket.

March

Monday, 2nd March

'Quick, quick,' said Holly, ushering me into the classroom this morning, 'the March and April hamster sign-up sheet is up!'

I ran over as fast as I could. There were still loads of spaces left on it and even better, there were week-long slots available during the Easter holidays. I remembered the pet show I saw advertised at judo, it was on 18th April. I checked the sheet and YES, that date was during the second week of the Easter holiday. I quickly signed up. This means I can enter the pet show after all. Hoooorrrraaaay!

'I'll get him for a whole week,' I said, my heart racing. My family normally goes camping during the Easter holiday so I'll have to make sure it doesn't clash with my week of looking after Fred, and the entry into the pet show.

I'm not sure if the pet show animal has to be your own pet. I suppose Fred is a class pet and as I will be looking after him, he is kind of my pet for the week. Yes, I think it'll be fine.

Tuesday, 3rd March

Last night I drew a plan of the obstacle course I'm going to make for Fred.

'Mum,' I said at teatime, 'you know that class hamster I told you about?'

'Yes,' said Mum.

'I'm looking after him for the second week of the Easter holidays.'

'Great,' said Mum, 'as long as you clean and feed him yourself.' She plonked a rather large piece of steaming broccoli on my plate. 'I've booked our camping trip for the first week so that second week is completely free.'

'Can I play with the hamster too?' asked Joppin.

'Of course you can,' said Mum.

After tea I went up to my room and cleared the top of my desk ready for the cage. I know there's about six weeks to go, but it's best to be prepared.

Friday, 6th March

Sarah's birthday is at the end of March and today she handed out party invitations. It's going to be a science party on Saturday, 29th March at the university.

'What's a science party?' asked Mandy as she studied her invitation.

'Oh, we're going to do experiments, create explosions, and make a rocket,' said Sarah, a large smile spreading across her face.

'Sounds good,' I said, briefly wondering if I could work a rocket into my pet routine then quickly deciding against it.

'So who's invited?' asked Holly.

'Well, you three of course, and three people from chess club, including Enid, my older person. I'm also inviting a few people from the Saturday technology club I've been going to.'

'Your older person is going! That is so brilliant,' said Holly.

That got me wondering about my older person project. I've decided to go round to see Mr Alimo on Sunday.

Saturday, 7th March

When I got to judo today, I went straight up to the pet show poster. The sign-up sheet was still there, phew! There was a space for your name, your pet's name, your email address and your phone number. I quickly filled in the spaces using my best purple pen. I felt all tingly, a mixture of excitement and nerves running through me. That's it! Fred and I are now officially going to be in a pet show! OH MY GOODNESS, I can't believe it! What's even more exciting is that at the bottom of the poster it said, 'PRIZES FOR EVERYONE'. Wow, now that is my kind of pet show! I wonder what I'll win. YIPPPPPEEE!

During judo we had to practise falling over. In judo when you fall over, you have to hit the ground as hard as you can with the whole length of your arm. This makes a loud crashing sound on the mat, which makes the fall seem much more dramatic than it really was.

We all lined up at the end to the lesson and Sensai Yoshi walked up and down the line.

'In two weeks,' he said, 'we will be having a competition. A club from Scunthorpe will be coming over for the day.' I shuddered at the thought of doing judo matches with people I didn't know. I hope they are all very, very small.

Sunday, 8th March
MR ALIMO

Mum and I walked to Mr Alimo's house after lunch.

'Why are you carrying a small pie?' I whispered.

'It's nice to take a gift when you visit someone,' she said.

We nervously approached the house and yes, he was in his garden as expected. As we got closer we noticed that several beanpoles were stuck into the soil and on the top of one of them was... the knitted

125

egg cosy Mum had brought last time. Mum looked at me and we both smiled.

'Hello there,' said Mum as we stopped by his wall.

'Oh hello,' said Mr Alimo. 'I'm just putting some potatoes in pots.'

'Great, I've brought you a pie,' said Mum, placing the small pie on the wall.

'Oh, what sort?' he asked, coming over.

'Potato pie,' said Mum.

'Oh.' Mr Alimo looked at the pie and then at the large pile of potatoes on the floor. 'So what can I do for you?'

Mum nudged me but I didn't know what to say. 'Maggie wants to ask you something.'

'Um,' I began, 'we're doing a project about um... old peop... um, about gardening in the olden days and I wondered if you could tell me about it.'

I don't know why I said that bit about gardening. I just couldn't say we had to find an old person for an older person project. I mean, Mr Alimo might not even think he's that old. Anyway, it worked because he looked delighted.

'I can do better than tell you about it, I can show you,' he said, dusting the soil off his fingers. 'First lesson next Sunday?' I nodded. 'Well, I need to get back to my jobs but I'll see you in a week, shall we say Sunday at 9 a.m. then?' he said.

We nodded. 'Thanks,' said Mum. She left the pie on the wall and we headed home.

Monday, 9th March

We had a drama lesson today. We each had to pretend to be our souvenir. I just crouched in a corner. Not the best lesson ever.

Wednesday, 11th March

It rained all day and we had to have playtime inside. During wet playtime we get out all sorts of board games and art equipment. Holly and I had a go at drawing hamsters, Mandy drew a girl wearing cowboy boots, and Sarah drew these amazing aliens.

'They look brilliant,' I said to Sarah, immediately trying to draw one.

'Enid showed me how to draw them. They key is to make the head and the eyes really big,' Sarah said.

We all started drawing aliens; Mandy put a dress and boots on hers.

'Your older person is pretty unusual teaching you how to draw aliens,' said Mandy.

'She's great,' said Sarah, 'she's actually seen a real alien.'

'Really?' asked Holly. We all looked at Sarah, waiting for more information.

'Yes, she was camping once, years ago. She was sitting outside her tent and there was a sudden flash of light. A few minutes later an alien ran past and disappeared.'

Quentin, who was hovering about nearby, shook

his head. 'As if! Everyone knows there's no such thing as aliens. You are so pathetic believing that rubbish.'

'My older person saw it, and older people don't lie,' said Sarah.

'Your older person is probably confused and stupid,' said Quentin, 'not like Bruce who is intelligent and interesting.'

Sarah gritted her teeth and turned away from Quentin, who eventually drifted away.

We carried on drawing aliens and coloured them in green. They looked really good.

I can't wait to meet Enid at Sarah's party, as she sounds so interesting. I wonder if Mr Alimo will have any amazing stories to tell. I suspect not. I think we'll mostly be talking about potatoes.

Saturday, 14th March

After judo Mum and I went to town to look for a present for Sarah's birthday.

We went to the Debenhams café for a drink and a piece of cake. (YUM!) Then we looked around lots of shops. I was struggling to find something good for Sarah though, and I was getting a bit worried as it was getting late. I knew that if I didn't find something soon, Mum would probably try and make her a homemade present later. Mum has made presents for my friends before and it's always sooooooo embarrassing.

'Time to go home,' said Mum eventually.

'Oh no!' I said, freezing with horror. I started frantically looking around and then I saw a really colourful shop. It had all sorts of comics, models from TV shows, lava lamps and other weird items in the window. Yippeee, there was hope! I pulled Mum's arm and we ran towards it. When we went inside, all the brilliant things on the shelves amazed me. I had a good look round and found the perfect present for Sarah. It was an inflatable alien, which was very like the ones we'd drawn at school.

P*E*R*F*E*C*T

I'm so excited about giving it to her. She's going to LOVE IT!!!!!!

I can't wait for the party now!!!

Sunday, 15th March
OLDER PERSON PROJECT

'Come on, Maggie, wake up!' said Mum as she came into my room and opened the curtains this morning. A little bit of sun tried to squeeze through the clouds.

'But it's Sunday,' I said, burying my head under my duvet.

'Yes, but we're visiting Mr Alimo this morning, remember?'

I was so cosy in my bed but I crawled out anyway as I knew I had to go. I was well behind with my older person project and really had to get started on it.

We had a quick breakfast, wrapped up warm, and set off. It was very cold outside and I really hoped Mr Alimo would invite us into his house and give us biscuits. When we arrived, we were very surprised to see that Mr Alimo was not in his garden as usual. We were even more surprised to see that Mum's pie from last week was still balanced on the wall looking very soggy.

'Oh no, something must have happened or he'd have eaten it,' said Mum, running to the door and knocking loudly.

Mr Alimo opened the door and smiled. 'Hello, ladies, we'll talk as we dig,' he said, handing me a gardening fork and Mum a spade. We had to dig up the soil, turn it over, and then put it back again. It took ages and I was shivering the whole time.

'March is the month of preparation,' he said. 'Prepare the ground and remove early weeds.' He picked a straggly shoot from the ground and threw it to one side; it landed on Mum's pie.

Eventually, we were invited in for a drink. My fingers were so cold I could hardly move them and I rubbed them together as I sat on one of his purple velvet chairs.

I drank homemade elderflower juice (interesting flavour) and Mum had a cup of tea. I was starting to warm up a bit and I began to look around the room, noticing all sorts of strange antiques, including an old brass telescope sitting next to the window.

Mr Alimo didn't talk much so we just sat really quietly having our drinks. I was a bit worried that I wouldn't have much to write about in my project notebook, but I decided I could describe the digging in some detail.

'Now, before you go I have something for you to do,' he said as he took our cups into the kitchen. He came back with a yogurt pot full of soil. I noticed there was a sticker on the pot that said 'MAGGIE'. 'Just make a hole with your finger,' he said, passing me the pot, 'then drop in this sunflower seed.'

I did as instructed and brushed the soil over the hole. I wasn't too sure what to do with my soily finger so I just put it in my pocket.

'I'll keep this seed safe for you then you can see how it's getting on during your visits,' said Mr Alimo, taking the pot and putting it on the window sill.

We arranged to return next Sunday to continue our gardening work. I hope we don't have to dig again.

I did some writing in my project notebook when I got back. I described the digging and talked about my cold fingers. I also wrote a bit about the antiques in Mr Alimo's house and drew a picture of the antique telescope.

Monday, 16th March
GRANDMA MERLE

'Of course you can visit again, Merle,' said Mum into her phone. 'Yes, we'll see you in three weeks.' She hung up and turned to Dad. 'I think we're going to have to start tidying up.'

It turns out that Grandma Merle is coming to stay again. It's not for a few weeks so hopefully we'll have time to get the house sorted out.

'Is she getting her flat painted again?' asked Joppin.

'She didn't say why she wanted to visit,' said Mum as she dusted the TV with a tissue, 'but I think she's lonely. She's been living on her own for five years and I think she finds it hard.'

'Please don't put the toilet seats under my bed again,' I said.

Less than two weeks to go until Sarah's party. I'm so excited about giving her the alien and I spent ages wrapping it in special space wrapping paper. It looks amazing. I looked out of the window earlier and wondered if aliens really could exist. Could Enid's story be true?

Friday, 20th March

'Let's talk a bit about our older person project,' said Mrs Perkins this morning. Sarah stood up and talked about Enid. She even told everyone the bit about the alien. I could see Quentin trying not to laugh.

'My older person,' said Quentin, 'doesn't need to make up silly stories about aliens because people already think he's interesting. He's travelled all over the world and met all sorts of fascinating people.' I could see Sarah deflate in her chair.

'How about you, Maggie?' said Mrs Perkins.

'Well, my older person, Mr Alimo, is teaching me about gardening.' Quentin let out a huge yawn.

'Interesting,' said Mrs Perkins.

At playtime Quentin came over. 'What a boring older person you've got,' he said to me, 'but at least he's not making up ridiculous stories about aliens.' He smirked and walked off, pointing to the sky.

'Well, I think she sounds brilliant,' I said. 'I can't wait to meet her.'

Sarah smiled.

When I got home, I suddenly realised that the judo competition with the other club is tomorrow!!!!!

Joppin and I got out the judo practice dummies and had a go at throwing them about. It looked really funny and we ended up giggling on the floor, trying to pin each other down using the strange-looking characters.

After tea I began to feel a bit nervous about the possibility of fighting scary unknown children. My stomach felt kind of loose inside. I sneaked behind the sofa and found Joppin's anti-bullying pompom jumper. I bundled it up and took it up to my room.

Yes, it was still full of pompoms, making it nicely padded. My plan is to wear the jumper under my judo suit to give me a bit of extra protection during the competition.

Finding the jumper has also reminded me that I need to sell more pompoms, as I need more money for the holiday fund.

Saturday, 21st March
JUDO COMPETITON

I WON A MEDAL!!!!!

I put the pompom jumper on under my judo suit. Not only was I protected, but I was also nice and warm.

All the kids from the other judo club were lined up on the other side of the mat and I noticed that many of them looked quite scary. My first fight was with a small girl who I managed to pin down straight away. This meant I was through to the next round.

My second fight was with a bigger girl who I accidentally tripped up without meaning to. This meant I was in the final!

I was rather nervous, as the last fight was against this huge girl who stared at me and snarled before making a fist and pounding it into her other hand. I started shaking all over and I suddenly felt very hot. I considered running away.

'*Hajimi*,' said Sensei Yoshi.

We began the fight. I was leaping about trying not to be tripped up or thrown as she tried to grab my suit. I was jumping around quite manically when suddenly one of the pompoms came loose and rolled out of my sleeve. The big girl suddenly stopped looking at me and watched the orange pompom fall and roll across the mat. At that moment I quickly turned and pulled her forward and did a good throw over my back.

She fell down flat and... I won!!! Everyone cheered.

I couldn't stop smiling as Sensai Yoshi put the medal over my head. Joppin had lost his first match so he wasn't even in the boys final. He wouldn't speak to me at all on the way home.

When we got back, I took two pompoms out of the jumper. I'm going to try and sell them next week.

Saturday, 28th March
SARAH'S SCIENCE PARTY

I'm just back from Sarah's science party, which was BRILLIANT.

At the beginning we all sat in a circle chatting while we waited for the 'mad scientist' to arrive.

'Hello, I'm Enid,' said the oldest woman I've ever seen. She had long white hair and she wore a floor-length black dress.

'Oh hello, I'm Maggie,' I said.

'Isn't this just so exciting,' she said as she smiled and looked around the room.

'Yes,' I said just as smoke started coming out of a bucket and collecting on the floor. The white lights went dark then green and red lights came on. We all sat on tall stools that were scattered around the area.

Suddenly, a young woman in a lab coat came running into the room. She stood amongst the foggy mist, next to a small table.

'Hi, I'm Professor Lucy Wilmot, welcome to the Mad Scientist show,' she said. 'First I'll do the show, then we'll have a party tea, and after that we'll make rockets and launch them outside... Sound good?'

'Yes!' everyone shouted.

She then showed us lots of experiments. Liquids exploded, bottles fizzed, tubes popped, and huge smoke rings rolled through the air. It was pretty amazing.

After the show we had the party tea in a different room.

'I love this party,' Holly said, as she chose several different biscuits from the buffet.

'It's good, isn't it?' said Sarah.

We filled our plates and sat at one of the high orange tables. I looked over and saw Enid with the chess club people. She was the centre of attention and seemed to be telling all sorts of funny stories.

After the party tea we went back to the main room and got into small groups to make the rockets. I was with Holly, Sarah and Mandy... yippee! We started making our rocket out of a plastic bottle, a cardboard cone, plastic tail wings, and a cork. We then half-filled it with water before taking it outside.

It was a clear night and I could see loads of stars in the dark sky. I shivered as I'd left my coat inside, and all the hairs on my arms stood up. The excitement and chill combined made me feel all strange and tingly.

We lined up the rockets and Lucy put a small red light on the nose of each one. The launching involved putting the rocket on a stand, then attaching a bike pump to the cork and pumping away. Ours was being launched first and we waited while everyone counted down. As we got to zero Professor Wilmot (Lucy) pulled a string, which released the rocket and it shot through the sky leaving a stream of red light behind it.

My heart was beating fast. Everyone was watching the rocket and cheering. It was AMAZING!

After the party Mandy, Holly and I went back to Sarah's for a sleepover. Her dad had decorated her house with science-themed items. There was test tube bunting, periodic table buns, and a Bunsen burner-shaped cake complete with yellow flame icing. (He'd made it all himself.)

After we'd had some cake Sarah opened her presents. When she opened mine, she screamed in delight.

'I LOVE it!' she said, pulling the alien from its box and starting to blow it up. When it was blown up, it looked really good, and she hugged it before dancing around the room holding its little green hands.

Holly gave her a chemistry set and Mandy gave her a 'make a robot' kit but I think mine was the favourite present. She even put it in its own sleeping bag when we all went to bed.

Monday, 30th March

Only four days until the Easter holidays. Everything has gone very Easterish at school. Mrs Perkins is making us write stories about our souvenir celebrating Easter (imagine a bonnet on an acorn), we're drawing Easter bunnies in art, and we're making Easter eggs in cookery. (Can't complain about that one.)

On Thursday (the last day of term) our class is going to be hiding Easter eggs around the playground so that the little kids in Reception and Year One can do an Easter egg hunt. This is quite a good idea but I would prefer it if our class was doing the hunting rather than the hiding.

Wednesday, 1st April

Oh dear, the Easter egg hunt didn't go that well! Our class was given lots of eggs to hide and I had the brilliant idea of putting one up a tree. The only problem was that the tree in the playground was pretty hard to climb so I threw my egg up and it landed quite high up, balanced between two branches.

Later on the little kids came running out, clutching their cardboard Easter baskets with excited smiles on their faces. We all stood around the edge watching them.

A very small boy saw my egg up in the tree and started jumping up and down. He then somehow managed to climb the tree by doing a sort of monkey shuffle up the trunk. He sat on a branch and ate the egg while waving at all the other kids below.

It was only when he decided it was time to come down that it became apparent there was a problem.

He couldn't get down and as soon as he realised, he started crying.

I rushed over but I couldn't reach him. Mr Walsh, the caretaker, couldn't reach him. Mr Winters, the tallest teacher in the school, couldn't reach him. In the end Mrs Foley had to ring the fire brigade. After about an hour four firemen managed to get him down. Oh dear!

Saturday, 4th April
EASTER HOLIDAYS

I'm going camping today. I don't like to take my diary camping, as I don't really want a record of something I hope to forget about when I'm older. So goodbye, diary, see you in one week.

Saturday, 11th April

I'm now back from camping. It wasn't so bad actually, except for day two when it snowed and day four when the tent leaked and my sleeping bag got very wet. Oh, and day six when a bug was found in my welly.

Sunday, 12th April

It was so lovely to sleep in my proper bed last night, so comfy and warm. I slept for twelve whole hours, which I think is a record for me.

'Come on, Maggie, we need to collect the hamster,' called Dad at 9 a.m. I rushed downstairs as it had been arranged that I would collect Fred from Claire's house.

I'm helping Mr Alimo with his garden this afternoon but I think I'll have a few hours to play with Fred before lunch.

LATER

Well, I didn't really get the chance to play with Fred before lunch because he was asleep. He did wake up after tea though so I had a good play with him then. I even set up some of the obstacle course items on my bedroom floor. He kept trying to go under my cupboard though, so I made a wall around the course using piles of books and old shoeboxes.

It went pretty well with Mr Alimo today. We did a bit of weeding then planted some seeds inside and put them on the windowsills. I was pleased to see that my sunflower had started to grow. After the planting Mum, Mr Alimo and I sat on the velvet chairs.

'The bleak winter makes the spring more wonderful,' he said, handing me a mug of juice and a biscuit. I wrote that down in my project notebook when I got home.

<u>Monday, 13th April</u>

There was a small problem last night and as a result I'm rather tired today. Fred kept going on his squeaky wheel every 20 minutes, which kept waking me up. Because of this I hardly got any sleep. YYYYAAAAAWWWWWNNNNN.

We moved him downstairs into the kitchen this morning, he's going to be living there for the rest of the week.

<u>Tuesday, 14th April</u>

OH MY GOSHY GOODNESS!!!

A lady from Bell Farm rang today. She was checking that Fred and I were still coming to the pet show on Saturday. Luckily, the show starts at 5.30 p.m. This seems quite late for a pet show but the lady said it's because they serve an evening meal to the audience. She's even reserved a table for my friends and family so I'm going to ring Holly and the others later to see if any of them can make it.

It's quite good that it's at 5.30 because there's a small chance Fred will be awake.

SOOOOO EXCITED!

Yippee... and the poster said 'Prizes for Everyone' - double yippee! I wonder what my prize will be. I wonder if Fred will get his own prize.

All that's left to do now is Fred training.

Friday, 17th April
PET SHOW TOMORROW!!!!!

Well, this week has been a frenzy of training Fred and helping Mum and Dad tidy up ready for Grandma Merle, who's coming on Sunday.

I rang the girls to see if they wanted to come to the pet show. Mandy's in America and Sarah's gone to Whitby, but Holly can make it and is coming here first to help get everything ready. It's going to be soooooooo brill. Mum, Dad and Joppin are coming along too.

I've been training Fred to do some tricks and he can now can run through a kitchen roll tube, go down a small ramp, carry a pompom while walking over a bridge, and go in a shoebox then pop up though a hole in the lid. Altogether I think our act is very entertaining and I hope to win one of the main prizes.

Saturday, 18th April
THE PET SHOW

'So,' said Holly, as she helped me pack up the cardboard tubes and boxes, 'how can we make sure Fred's awake for the show?'

We looked in his cage and saw that he was huddled up asleep in the little wooden house.

'I know,' I said, suddenly leaping up. 'If we put a dark sheet over the cage before the show, he might think it's the night, he always wakes up when it gets dark. We just need to keep the sheet over until the show to keep him awake.'

'You are a genius,' said Holly, as I rushed off to find something suitable.

'Come on, girls,' shouted Mum, 'I've found the address on my phone and it's 30 minutes away so we'll have to go in five minutes.'

We quickly got all the things we needed then put the cage in the car and carefully put the sheet over the top of it.

After lots of driving along country roads we saw a sign. It said 'Bell Farm – **Dog Centre**'!!!!

'I didn't know it was a dog centre,' said Dad.

'No, me neither,' I said.

'It looks nice though,' said Holly as we drove up a long drive to a huge house with beautifully tended gardens.

We saw several people walking up the drive and milling around the car park. Each person was accompanied by at least one dog.

'I think there'll be quite a few dogs in the show,' said Mum.

I desperately looked at everyone, hoping to see another hamster, a cat, even a pet snail... but no, the only animals I could see were dogs.

Dogs

Dogs

Dogs

Dogs

Everywhere.

I began to feel the blood pumping around my body. I heard the squeak of Fred's wheel in the boot of the car as we pulled into a parking space.

'I'm not sure I want to go,' I mumbled.

'It'll be great,' said Dad, getting the covered cage out of the car and handing it to me.

I was extremely glad that the sheet was covering the cage; perhaps people would think it was a small dog in a carrying box.

Mum, Dad and Joppin went to look around the gardens while Holly and I went into the house. As we carried the cage inside I kept looking around for animals other than dogs. I didn't see any.

'Hello,' said a woman carrying a clipboard, 'who are you?'

'Um, Maggie and Fred,' I said.

'Oh yes,' she said, looking at a list. 'Welcome to the Bell Farm Dog Show. You're on table three, just keep Fred at the table until you're called.'

DOG SHOW??????????

I stared at Holly in shock. With quivering hands I carried Fred into the hall and hid the cage, still covered, under the table.

'You never said it was a dog show,' whispered Holly.

'I didn't know,' I said.

The large room was filling up fast and there were dogs everywhere. The sound of excited chatter filled the room and a strong smell of dog wafted around.

'I think we'll have to leave,' I said, looking around.

Just then Mum, Dad and Joppin came in. Mum was carrying the bag full of toilet roll tubes and pompoms. I looked at the stage; it had a huge ramp, a big see-saw, a large tunnel and some hurdles on it.

I felt sick as Mum handed me the small bag and sat down.

'What a great atmosphere!' said Mum.

'Mum,' I said, 'I think we need to leave.'

'Nonsense, we've just got here.'

'I think it's a dog show,' I said.

Mum looked around the room then looked back at me. 'Well, we're here now,' she said.

Just then a woman came onto the stage and called up the first dog and owner. A woman with a large poodle went up. The dog did all sorts of tricks like rolling over and jumping over the hurdles. I noticed there was a proper TV cameraman filming it. He was quite near us so we couldn't talk. I was very aware of the squeak coming from Fred's wheel.

Everyone applauded as the woman and the large poodle finished and another person was called up.

I was desperately trying to think of a way to get out of the situation. I considered fainting or escaping from the room unseen. I was just working out the best route to crawl out of the hall when I heard something that made every fibre of my body freeze.

'And next, Maggie and Fred.'

My mouth went dry and I couldn't move.

'Come on, Maggie,' said Mum, getting the sheet-covered cage out from under the table and handing it to me. I walked up to the front and put the cage on the stage. I was just about to explain about the terrible misunderstanding when the woman with the microphone pulled off the sheet.

There was Fred looking out of the cage. Everyone in the audience started laughing. The man with the camera came right up to the cage and started filming us.

'Oh, um, what a dear little thing,' said the woman. 'Well, this is most unusual; we've never had a hamster in the dog show before.' The audience was falling about in hysterics. 'But you're welcome to try the obstacles.'

I got Fred out and put him at the bottom of the see-saw. He ran up but was too light to tip it once he got past the middle, so I very slowly tipped it for him. Next were the hurdles. Fred just sat at the bottom of the hurdles sniffing around. I gently picked him up and placed him on the other side of the hurdles, and everyone clapped.

The tunnel was next. Fred ran in and it was all looking quite promising. However, he didn't come out again so I had to crawl in after him. He'd found a rubber ball in there and was busy trying to chew it. I guided him out.

After that I put him on top of the table and gave him a pompom, which he happily carried around. Everyone was clapping. Then, as I put him back in his cage, everyone started cheering and some people stood up. Fred went on his wheel and I carried him back to the table.

'Well, that was very good, very funny,' said the woman, before calling up the next person.

Everyone was looking over to our table. My heart was thumping loudly but the relief that it was over flooded my body and I sat back to enjoy the rest of the show and the rather tasty hot dogs that were being brought round.

'Brilliant, just brilliant,' said the cameraman, giving me a smile.

At the end of the evening the prizes were given out. I came 17th and my prize was a large plastic bone... hmmmmmm.

'That was so funny,' said the lady who hosted the show as we were on our way out. 'I think you may have provided some great publicity for Bell Farm Dog Centre, thank you.' She patted me on the back.

'Well, I think it went quite well,' said Mum on the way home.

'Yours was the best act,' said Holly.

'Why did you enter a hamster in a dog show?' asked Joppin.

I sighed and explained once again that I didn't know it was a dog show.

Sunday, 19th April

Guess what?!?!?! Fred and I were on the local news!!!!!!!!!! There was a section about the dog show.

'An unusual entry into the annual dog show,' said the presenter, before showing the film of Fred running into the tube then me crawling in after him.

Mum, Dad and Joppin all looked at each other then laughed.

Most of the afternoon was taken up with tidying ready for the arrival of Grandma Merle late tonight.

We briefly popped in to see Mr Alimo.

'Sorry we can't stay longer,' said Mum to Mr Alimo as we did a spot of weeding, 'but my mother is coming to stay and we need to get everything ready.'

'Oh, bring her round next week,' said Mr Alimo.

'Oh, okay, I'll mention it,' said Mum. 'I'm not sure she's the gardening type though.'

Monday, 20th April
BACK TO SCHOOL

As I carried Fred into school a huge crowd gathered around us. It seems that almost everyone had seen the news, and those who hadn't had seen the whole thing on YouTube.

'Can I have your autograph?' asked a boy from Year One.

'Um, yes, later,' I said, rushing into the classroom.

Mrs Perkins was there. I was worried I'd be in trouble for entering the class pet into a competition, but she said it was funny. She'd even made a little medal to hang on Fred's cage - phew!

'My famous granddaughter,' said Grandma Merle when I got home. She stood up and gave me a loose hug. 'Now come and tell me the whole story.'

I told Grandma Merle all about the misunderstanding and she nodded throughout.

'Always check the facts,' she said.

'Um, yes, thanks, Grandma,' I said.

After that we looked on YouTube. The film of Fred and me has been viewed 18,000 times!!

I told Grandma about Mr Alimo too and how he wanted to meet her. She looked quite pleased and asked lots of questions about him. I pointed out his house and she seemed quite impressed with the garden.

Tuesday, 21st April

Today Jake asked me if I had any hamster pompoms. This has given me the brilliant idea of selling hamster pompoms. I started planning it all tonight. I'm going to make several orange-and-white pompoms onto which I will glue googly eyes and cardboard teeth. They should look pretty good.

Wednesday, 22nd April

'Have you seen Grandma Merle?' asked Mum when I got back from school. It turns out that Grandma has been missing all day.

Dad sat sick with worry, while Mum looked all around the neighbourhood.

Finally, at 9 p.m. she arrived home.

'Where have you been?' asked Mum.

'I'm a grown woman,' said Grandma. 'I can go out and look after myself,' she said, before going to bed.

Saturday, 25th April

Something very strange is going on. Grandma Merle was due to go back to her own home tomorrow but she's now staying for an extra week. Also, she keeps disappearing for several hours at a time.

Hmmmmmmmmm... mysterious.

Sunday, 26th April
Mr Alimo

We went to see Mr Alimo today. We asked
Grandma Merle if she wanted to come but she
decided to go into town shopping instead.

'Hello,' said Mum as we got to Mr Alimo's house.
She handed him some gardening mittens she'd made
out of felt.

'Oh hello,' he said brightly as he took the mittens
and put them in the greenhouse. He had several
pieces of wood in the front garden. 'We're making
some vegetable troughs,' he said, running his hand
along one of the planks. 'Woodwork is like gardening,
it's about catching nature and moulding it.'

For the next three hours we helped to make large
boxes out of wood. I even did some sawing, which
was quite hard but fun. My favourite job was
hammering the nails in though, and it turns out that
I'm rather good at it. Eventually, two large boxes sat
in the garden.

'Let's celebrate with a drink,' he said as we all
went inside to wash our hands. We took our drinks
through to the lounge ready to sit on the velvet
chairs. It was then that I saw it in the corner of the
room. I nudged Mum and pointed to it. She stared at

me, her mouth open. There in the corner of the room was... Grandma Merle's hat.

'Yes, Mr Alimo and I have met and we are now good friends,' said Grandma when we asked her about it later. 'I told him I was your Grandma and he invited me in straight away.'

'Is that why you want to stay longer?' asked Mum.

'Might be,' said Grandma.

Tuesday, April 28th

Yippee! I managed to sell all six of the hamster pompoms I made and now I have £30.05 in the holiday fund. I checked the Travel Hotel website and the cheapest room is £39, so it looks like I really could make enough for a one night stay. It will be AMAZING if I can book, pay for, and take my family to a real hotel.

Friday, 1st May

'I'm going to give you another chance,' said Mrs Perkins this morning. YES, we're going to have another go at making a school newspaper. 'But this time,' she continued, 'everything is going to be carefully checked by me, and girls,' she pointed to me, Holly, Mandy and Sarah, 'you will be doing the maths quiz. I don't think you can cause too much trouble with that.'

I'm very glad there's going to be a new school newspaper, as I felt a bit bad about what happened before, but I kind of wish we were doing cartoons or the cover design. Maths quiz isn't really my thing.

'Isn't it great that we get to do the maths quiz!' said Sarah at playtime. We sighed.

The newspaper will be given out at the end of term, which gives us quite a long time to come up with questions.

Peter, Jake and a couple of the other boys are doing a special newspaper report on the older person

157

project. Quentin is doing general news and Claire and her friends are doing jokes.

'The most interesting older person project will feature on the cover,' said Mrs Perkins. 'We could even have a photo of the winner of best project, with his or her older person, on the front.'

'That'll be my project,' said Quentin. 'I can just see it now, a photo of me and Bruce and an article about how much I've helped him.

Saturday, 2nd May

At judo today we practised throwing someone over our back. It's quite difficult as you have to get them off-balance, bend your knees, turn and pull all at the same time.

After judo I got the judo practice dummy out from under my bed and practised with it. It was actually all right and I threw it over my back loads of times.

Sunday, 3rd May

'Let me stay just one more week,' said Grandma Merle today. It turns out that she doesn't want to go home. It also turns out that she's been going to Mr Alimo's house every day.

She even accompanied us when we went round to see him today. As we arrived Mr Alimo ran up to Grandma Merle and gave her a piece of purple broccoli. She smiled broadly as she accepted it and sat on the little bench he'd put beside the front door.

We spent much of the morning filling the wooden boxes with soil. Then we planted some seeds in little trays from the greenhouse.

'Now that the risk of frost is over,' said Mr Alimo to me, 'we need to bring your sunflower outside.' He asked me and Mum to move a very large pot and put it next to the bench. 'I'd do it myself but I'm not as strong as I used to be.'

Mum and I moved the pot and filled it with soil. Then Mr Alimo got my little sunflower, which was just a stem with three small leaves on it, and we transferred it from the yogurt pot into the large pot. Next he got a long garden cane, put one of Mum's homemade mittens on the top, then put it next to the little plant.

'This will support it as it grows,' he said.

'It looks lovely,' said Grandma Merle, watching from the bench. 'A handy stick too,' she added, pointing to the mitten. Mr Alimo laughed as if it was the funniest thing he had ever heard.

<u>Tuesday, 5th May</u>

Today we worked on our newspaper jobs. Sarah had brought in several printouts of maths quiz questions she'd found on the Internet.

'Shall we try and make it funny?' I asked.

'How can a maths quiz be funny?' asked Mandy.

'I don't know, maybe we could have funny questions like what is half of eight? And the answer could be zero because if you cut an eight in half across the middle it kind of looks like two zeros, you know, on top of each other.'

There was a rather long silence.

'I've got one,' said Sarah. 'When I add five to nine, I get two. The answer is correct, but how?'

'I don't know, what's the answer?' asked Holly.

'When it's 9 a.m. Add five hours to 9 a.m. and you get 2 p.m.,' said Sarah.

We all agreed that it was sort of good so now we've got our very first quiz question. I kind of think my half of eight question was better but no one else seems to agree… strange.

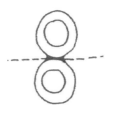

Sunday, 10th May

Grandma Merle's going home today but she's coming back in a few weeks to visit again. It turns out she wants to spend a lot more time with Mr Alimo. I'm not sure if she's sort of moving in with us or not. I saw Mum looking on the Internet at local flats to let so she may be getting her own place.

I've been trying to think of ways to make a bit more money for the holiday fund, as I'm still £9 short. I've got this idea, which is to make pompom knee protectors. I've sewn a pompom onto a loop of elastic. The loop then goes over the knee with the pompom sitting over the kneecap. The idea is that if the wearers fall over, they'll be perfectly protected. I'm going to wear a pair under my trousers today, just to check they're comfy. The only problem is that they make my knees look extremely knobbly.

Monday, 11th May
EXCITING SCHOOL TRIP ALERT

'In exactly four weeks,' said Mrs Perkins this morning, 'you will all be going on a three-day school trip.' Everyone cheered. Once the noise died down Mrs Perkins continued. 'It is a survivalist trip so you will be learning how to survive in the great outdoors.'

'I already know how to survive anything,' said Quentin. 'Surviving outdoors is easy for me. I don't mind skinning a rabbit or anything.'

'Ewwwwwwww!' said Mandy. 'I'm not doing that.'

'Very good, Quentin,' said Mrs Perkins, 'you can give everyone tips then.'

'I can dig wells, tell the time by looking at shadows, everything,' he continued.

Everyone sighed.

It turns out that we're going to this place called Balby Forest. We're going to make shelters out of sticks and then sleep in them. And we'll learn how to make a fire and forage for food. Luckily, there was

162

no mention of rabbits.

'I hope I can take my phone,' said Mandy as we all sat down at the picnic table.

'I don't think that's really in the spirit of living in the wild,' said Sarah.

'Hmmmmm,' she said. 'Well, I'm definitely wearing my cowboy boots.'

'Let's tell scary stories around the fire,' said Holly.

'Let's do maths quizzes in the shelter,' said Sarah. We all raised our eyebrows then laughed.

'Why don't you make up silly stories about aliens?' said Quentin, wandering over.

'Ohhhh, we might see one!' I said.

'Ridiculous,' said Quentin, before running off tapping his head.

Thursday, 14th May

Oh dear, the pompom knee protectors weren't quite the hit I'd hoped. I wore them today to show everyone how they worked, then at lunchtime I got called to Mrs Foley's office where I was told off for making fun of Mr Walsh (the caretaker). It turns out he has naturally very knobbly knees. Who knew?

I didn't manage to sell any knee protectors at all so I'm now trying to think of another way to sell the pompoms.

163

Sunday, 17th May

'Hello, Mr Alimo,' Mum and I said as we arrived at his house ready for our afternoon of gardening.

'Oh hello,' he said, coming out of his house. He looked kind of sad and deflated. 'When is Merle back?' he asked.

'Um, next weekend I think,' said Mum.

'Great.'

We spent the afternoon planting small plants from the greenhouse trays into the large wooden boxes. Mr Alimo seemed to cheer up a bit and started talking about Merle.

I went to the bathroom at Mr Alimo's house and was very surprised to see a large towel covering the toilet.

Tuesday, 19th May

Today we wrote in our older person project books. Mine was pretty empty except for the drawing of the old telescope, a paragraph about digging, and the odd quote.

'Think about what you've learnt from your older person,' said Mrs Perkins. I sat quietly. Quentin was scribbling away, Sarah had a big smile on her face as she drew aliens in her book, and even Mandy seemed to have lots to write about. I was trying to think of something. I guess I'd learnt how to make a wooden box and how to plant seeds. Then I thought about my sunflower and how watering it and looking after it had made it grow. Then I thought about how it felt kind of good to help Mr Alimo and keep him company on a weekend afternoon. Perhaps looking after people makes them grow too. I wrote it down as it sounded like the sort of think Mrs Perkins would like.

Thursday, 21st May

'If we were dropped in the woods with no food or water, I would easily survive but I doubt any of you would,' said Quentin at playtime. He sat down at the picnic table with us so we knew he wanted to carry on talking about it.

'I think I'd do okay,' said Mandy. 'I'd ring my dad or Pizza Hut.'

'Phones don't work in the real wild,' said Quentin.

'I'd eat bugs,' said Sarah.

'Yeah, some bugs are edible, I know which ones,' Quentin replied. 'Well if you need help during the trip, just ask me. The most important thing to remember is never panic.'

Just then the bell went and we managed to escape. Phewwwwww!

Sunday, 24th May

Grandma Merle came back today. She was wearing new clothes and she'd had her hair cut. When she came in, she gave me and Joppin some sweets– pear drops... YUM!

'I'm looking round a nearby flat this afternoon,' Grandma announced.

'You're moving near here?' I asked.

'Of course, I want to be near my lovely family.' She smiled at Joppin and me.

We all had an enormous Sunday lunch cooked by Dad, and I decided it would be quite nice to have Grandma living nearby.

Monday, 25th May

Grandma has just found a flat and is moving in in a few weeks. It's in walking distance from here and it's specially designed for older people. She's pretty excited and she even said Joppin and I can help to paint it. She's going to stay with us until the move, but she's out at Mr Alimo's house most of the time nowadays.

Friday, 29th May

Jake is taking photos of people with their older person as part of his newspaper assignment. I asked Mr Alimo if he minded and he said he'd love to be in the photo, so Jake is coming to Mr Alimo's house during our visit on Sunday. It's going to be very weird having him there.

I just hope he doesn't start talking about toilets or bottoms, especially if Grandma Merle is around.

Well, I must go now as I've got to practise judo with the dummy ready for the lesson tomorrow. I've got my yellow belt judo exam in three weeks. Eeeeeeeeek!

Sunday, 31st May

Well, Jake came and took the photos today. Grandma Merle was there too, so he took some of Mr Alimo, Grandma Merle and me all squashed up on the little bench.

He was very interested to hear that Grandma Merle and Mr Alimo met because of my doing the project. He wrote lots of notes in a notebook and I've got a feeling he's going to mention it in the article.

Monday, 1st June

ONLY ONE WEEK TO GO UNTIL THE SURVIVAL TRIP!!!

'Look at the book Enid lent me,' said Sarah at playtime. She got this large book out of her bag. It said 'UFOs and Aliens' on the cover. We looked at all these different drawings of spaceships and aliens. 'I wonder if we'll see any aliens on the trip,' I said.

'You will because...' Sarah beckoned us all in closer and whispered, 'you remember the rockets we made at the party... Well I'm thinking of launching a rocket, with the inflatable alien tied to it, while we're on the trip.'

'That will look brilliant,' said Holly.

'But don't tell anyone,' whispered Sarah, 'it'll be best if it's a surprise.'

We all giggled away and decided to call the plan 'PROJECT SECRET LAUNCH'.

'What's this book?' asked Quentin, coming over. He picked it up. 'Oh, a book for weirdos,' he said, flicking through it. 'It is so sad that some people actually believe this nonsense.' He threw the book down. 'Mumbo jumbo,' he shouted as he walked off.

Sunday, 7th June

The survival trip is tomorrow and I can't stop thinking about it. I've packed my bags and even sneaked in a packet of biscuits for a midnight feast. I can't imagine what it's going to be like. It's so strange to think that I'll be sleeping outside tomorrow night!!!

Thursday, 11th June
JUST BACK FROM THE TRIP

On Monday morning we all boarded the rickety orange bus and set off for Balby Forest. It was a bumpy ride along country lanes and we were all talking non-stop about our ideas for surviving in the wild.

It seemed to take a very long time but eventually we saw a sign that said 'Balby Forest – a Wild Adventure'. Everyone cheered as the bus turned off the road and eventually shuddered to a stop next to a large wooden shed. We all got off and grabbed our bags. The shed door was open so Mrs Perkins suggested we wait in there.

We were just starting to sit on benches inside the wooden building when a man jogged in and stood at the front. 'Helloooooo, I'm Mr Trimble,' he said as he jumped up and down. Mr Trimble had extremely long smooth hair, enormous muscley arms, and trousers with lots and lots of pockets. I'm sure I could see a hairbrush sticking out of one of the side pockets.

'I'm your survival skills leader,' he said, flicking his hair behind his shoulder. 'The first thing we need to do is make our shelters for tonight.' He then talked about different ways to make shelters using sticks, branches and trees. After the talk we all jogged behind him into the forest. Holly, Mandy, Sarah and I decided to make a big joint shelter. We collected loads of sticks and it was quite fun putting them all together to make a kind of tunnel. Mr Trimble helped us quite a bit with the tying because we couldn't quite reach the top. After that we put leafy branches over the sticks. When it was finished, we crawled inside. It was like a cosy little cave and we smiled as we sat amongst the leaves in our little foresty den.

We then went back to the wooden building to get our bags. Once our sleeping bags were neatly laid out inside the shelter it felt like a proper woodland house. It was a bit of a squash but that kind of added to the atmosphere.

We were starting to get a bit hungry and I was rather worried that we'd have to catch a rabbit to eat, but when we all assembled around Mr Trimble's campfire later, we were relieved to see there was a big box of Pot Noodles and lots of bottles of water. There was also a kettle ready to go on a hook that hung over the fire.

'Of course,' said Mr Trimble, gesturing for us to sit on logs that were lying around the fire, 'you wouldn't normally get Pot Noodles and bottled water in the wild, but let's pretend, eh?'

I could hear Quentin tutting behind me.

'And even though we have bottled water, we're going to filter it,' Mr Trimble continued, 'just so you can see how it's done.'

Mr Trimble then sat down and took off one of his enormous boots. He then peeled a damp sock off his rather grubby foot, a strange sweaty smell spread over the group.

'Right,' he said grabbing the kettle, 'you can use fabric to filter out the largest particles from the water.' He got a bottle of water, took off the lid, and put the smelly sock over it! We all watched in horror as he poured the water through the sock straight into the kettle.

I looked at Holly, who was staring at the kettle with her mouth open. Mandy pulled a sickened face and Sarah just put her head in her hands. Mr Trimble 'filtered' four more bottles through his sock while everyone watched, mortified.

'Who wants a Pot Noodle first?' he asked as he sat down and put his wet sock back on. Everyone was silent. Mr Trimble then put the kettle on the hook and asked us to keep an eye on it while he went to get some doughnuts. Once he was out of sight Jake quickly poured the water out of the kettle and replaced it with fresh clean water. Phew! (Jake got a lot of high fives for that.)

We all enjoyed our Pot Noodles and doughnuts. Well, all except Quentin who said he'd been looking forward to catching his dinner.

Sleeping in the shelter was really strange. I was aware of every little sound... leaves blowing in the wind, twigs snapping, other people moving about. It gave me goose bumps. Eventually, I got to sleep but I woke up loads of times.

On Tuesday we went for a long walk and picked some wild strawberries, which seemed to be growing in suspiciously straight rows.

But... the most amazing thing happened on Wednesday evening, the evening of OPERATION SECRET LAUNCH.

After tea (sandwiches with cheese made from the milk of the local wild cow) we all sat outside our shelters. We made sure no one could see us then

Sarah got out the rocket. She had it all prepared and had brought a bike pump and everything. We all giggled quietly as she blew up the alien and tied it to the rocket. It was starting to get dark and we knew we had to act quickly as this would be our last chance to do it during the trip.

We set up the rocket and Holly pumped away. After a couple of minutes of pumping Sarah pulled the release string and the rocket, closely followed by the alien, shot up into the air. It was really fast and it headed towards an area thick with trees. 'Aaaaaaaagh!'

We all jumped as we heard a scream from the next shelter. Suddenly, we saw Quentin leaping up. 'I don't believe it,' he said, before running into the woods at high speed pointing at the sky.

'Oh no!' said Sarah, 'he could get lost.'

Mandy started laughing so much that she started crying. Sarah rushed off to find Mr Trimble, who was by the communal fire. 'Quentin just ran right into the middle of the forest,' she said incredibly quickly. Mr Trimble immediately got up and sprinted towards the area shouting, 'Quentin!'

We all sat anxiously by the fire, waiting to see if they would return.

After about 30 minutes we saw Mr Trimble coming out of the forest. He had something under his arm. As he got closer we could see what he was carrying. It was Quentin, his arms and legs flapping around. Mr Trimble brought him back to the fire and sat him on one of the logs.

'I can't believe it, I've seen an... alien,' said Quentin, his face very pale and his voice very high. 'I need to go home, I don't feel well.'

Sarah looked down. 'It was a pretend alien,' she said.

'You saw it too?' he muttered.

'It was an inflatable alien, we did it,' said Sarah.

'No, the one I saw was real. I think it communicated with me.' He closed his eyes. 'It put strange images into my mind.'

Mr Trimble took Quentin back to the wooden building and arranged for his mum to collect him. Oh dear!

Friday, 12th June

Quentin's off school so we haven't seen him since the alien incident. Everyone's talking about it though, someone even said he'd been abducted and taken to a spaceship.

'I still feel bad about Quentin,' said Sarah at playtime.

'Well, you did tell him it was inflatable,' said Holly.

'Serves him right for making fun of Enid,' said Mandy.

'I know, but I still feel bad.'

We all assured Sarah that it wasn't her fault; she chewed her lip and looked worried though.

Sunday, 14th June

Joppin and I now have yellow belts. The judo grading went really well. All that practising with the dummies paid off.

Monday, 15th June

Quentin's still off.

Thursday, 18th June

QUENTIN'S BACK!!!

'I've been communicating with aliens,' he said as he walked into the classroom this morning, 'that's why I haven't been at school.'

'But you don't believe in aliens,' said Mandy laughing.

'Laugh all you want but I'm the special one they chose to have contact with, probably because of my great intelligence.'

A few people actually seemed to believe him and asked him what happened.

'I can't say much,' he said. 'The government has asked me to keep quiet about it as they don't want the public to panic.'

Just then Mrs Perkins walked in.

'Remember,' she said, 'only one week until the older person projects have to be handed in.' She sat on her desk. 'Now,' she continued, 'we haven't done any work about our souvenirs recently, have we?'

So for the next hour I had to write a poem to my souvenir. Hmmmmmmm, not the easiest task ever. Here's what I came up with:

To My Acorn

By Maggie Moore

Oh wrinkled one,
You are so small.

You're drying up,

You are not tall. (I know I know... not very good, but I was desperate for something that rhymed with small.)

You haven't become an oak tree,

But perhaps you will, we will see.

I suspect you probably won't,

A good animal is a goat. (Not quite a rhyme but near enough.)

Mrs Perkins once said, 'there's no such thing as a bad poem'. This is good news because it means that my poem might not be as bad as it seems.

Sunday, 21st June

We helped Grandma Merle move into her new flat today. It's actually quite nice and she seemed pleased with it. Straight after she'd moved in she went round to Mr Alimo's house though. In fact, we all went round. It was a good visit today because some of the things we've been growing were ready for picking.

We picked beans, lettuces, strawberries and gooseberries. Then Grandma Merle cooked a meal using the ingredients and we all ate at Mr Alimo's house. Even Dad and Joppin were invited round. It was really busy but brilliant.

Monday, 22nd June

Aliens seem to be the big new trend at school. Everyone's talking about them and I've decided to make some alien characters with green pompom heads and pipe cleaner bodies. I think this could really bump up the holiday fund so I've been working hard and have already made four.

'You need to start thinking about your birthday party,' said Mum after tea. My birthday is in three weeks so I guess it's time to start planning. I told her I wanted an alien party just for my best friends and me, and she came up with the brilliant idea of going to the Planetarium. This is like a cinema where they project space and stars onto the ceiling. I leapt about in excitement as this is the perfect idea. I'm going to invite Holly, Sarah and Mandy to the Planetarium then back to mine for an alien-themed party tea and sleepover. Soooooooooo excited!

Tuesday, 23rd June

I made five more pompom aliens today... Whaaaaahooooooo! I'm going to take them to school to sell on Friday. Some people have already given me the money!!!

Wednesday, 24th June

Oh no, I've been so busy making aliens and writing the party invitations that I forgot about the older person project. This means that I had to do loads of work on it today.

Luckily, Dad had taken some photos of the meal on Sunday so I printed them off and glued them in. I also wrote about the gardening and about Grandma Merle and Mr Alimo becoming friends.

Friday, 26th June

Today I handed out the party invitations and I handed in my older person project. The girls are so excited about the party.

I also managed to sell all eight alien models. This means that I now have £39.05 in the holiday fund, which is enough for one night at the Birmingham Travel Hotel.

YIPPPPPPEEEEEE!

Mum helped me book it and Mum, Dad, Joppin and I will all be staying for one night in a family room at the end of July. I'm so proud that I've earned the money to take my family on holiday. YEEEEEEEHHHHAAAAAAAA! Joppin is very excited too and he keeps following me around doing his pigeon dance and saying 'thank you'.

Wednesday, 1st July

'This is a photo of me and Bruce,' said Quentin this morning. He was holding up a picture of him and Bruce (his older person) standing next to a very expensive looking convertible car. Bruce was holding a bottle of champagne and Quentin was holding a twenty-pound note. I sighed as I knew this would probably be the picture that would go on the front of the newspaper and if it was, Quentin would keep showing off about it.

Jake went over to have a look. 'Quite good,' he said, taking the picture and putting it in his 'article' folder.

Everything for the paper has to be in on Friday so we spent the afternoon working on our maths quiz. The good news is that my question (what is half of eight? – zero) is going to be in the quiz.

'We're desperate,' said Sarah. 'We've only got one question so we'll have to put Maggie's in.'

'Thanks,' I said.

We went on the Internet and found a few more good questions. In the end we have six, which I think is plenty.

- *If you have 9 and you add 5, you get 2, but how?*
- *What is half of 8?* (Waaahooo!)
- *What happened to the plant in the maths class?*
- *How do you make 7 even?*
- *Why is 6 afraid of 7?*
- *What is 27 multiplied by 82?* (I know, a bit dull, but Sarah made us put this one in.)

Answers

- *2 p.m.*
- *0*
- *It grew square roots*
- *Take away the 's'*
- *Because 7 8 9*
- *2,214.*

Friday, 10th July

Well, all the newspaper articles, art and quizzes are in and Mrs Perkins is checking them over the weekend before sending them to the printers. The paper is going to be out next Wednesday, which is quite exciting. I hope everyone likes the quiz.

Quentin is still going on about the alien thing. He said that the government keeps ringing him up to talk about his experience. He now says he was abducted and taken to a spaceship and that's why it took Mr Trimble so long to find him. He even asked Sarah if he could borrow her book about UFOs.

Hmmmmmmmm.

Sarah told him again that the alien he saw was an inflatable one but he won't listen. 'You're just jealous,' he said, 'because they chose me to connect with and not you.'

Sunday, 12th July

My actual birthday is tomorrow and there's less than a week to go until my party next Saturday. -
YIPPPPPEEEEE!

Mr Alimo and Grandma Merle came to our house for lunch today. It was strange because Mr Alimo hasn't been here before. It went really well though and he loved the garden. He even had a go on the monkey bars. There was nowhere to sit outside though as the toilet seat chairs are hidden away in the garage, and now that Grandma lives nearby they will probably stay there forever.

'Let's make some garden seats,' said Mr Alimo to Dad. 'I've got lots of wooden planks at home.'

'Great idea,' said Dad, before taking Mr Alimo for a tour of his shed.

Monday, 13 July

Happy birthday to me!!

Everyone sang happy birthday to me at lunchtime which was mega embarrassing, I'm not sure why.

My friends have agreed to give me my presents at my party next weekend so I just had the presents from my family to open today.

Mum and Dad gave me a homemade spacesuit made from old clothes covered in foil. It's awful and I know I can never wear it, but I smiled politely. Joppin gave me a homemade space helmet made from a woolly hat covered in foil, which is also awful. Grandma Merle and Mr Alimo gave me a small gold toilet-shaped penholder.

Noooooooooooo!

'Oh, thank you,' I said, wondering how quickly I could get rid of it.

'We accept you for who you are,' said Grandma. Hmmmmmmm.

Wednesday, 15th July
THE SCHOOL NEWSPAPER IS OUT

'They're here!' said Mrs Perkins as she struggled into the classroom carrying a large box. She dropped it with a thud onto her desk. 'It looks pretty good,' she said, opening the box and getting out a copy. She held it up and I couldn't believe it. The photo on the front cover was the one of me, Mr Alimo and Grandma Merle sitting on the bench. The headline said, 'School Project Brings People Together'. I felt the corners of my mouth turning up.

'It should have been me on the front,' said Quentin.

'Maggie's story was so lovely,' said Mrs Perkins. 'I was really touched.'

She handed out the papers and we all started looking through them. The middle pages were all about the older person project and I was pleased to see a large photo of Sarah and Enid playing chess in the centre.

'The picture of me is tiny!' shouted Quentin, pointing to a small picture of him and Bruce in the corner, 'and it's just our faces, where's the car?'

'Oh yes,' said Mrs Perkins, 'I trimmed it slightly, after all the project was about people not cars.'

I could hear Quentin huffing and sighing loudly behind me. 'I'll be telling my mum about this,' he said, before rolling up his newspaper and hitting the table with it.

Oh dear!

What made things even worse was that the news story that Quentin had written (about his alien abduction) had been shortened to two sentences and put on the back page.

Friday, 17th July
LAST DAY OF SCHOOL

We had a school end of term party today, which was quite fun. There were plates of sausage rolls and biscuits. It was good but I was busy thinking about my own party tomorrow.

After school I helped Mum make party decorations. She made aliens out of balloons, which were basically green balloons with tissue paper bodies and big eyes stuck onto them. We also made alien bunting by folding green paper and cutting out an alien shape. When the paper was opened, there was a string of aliens holding hands.

Dad had made an alien cake, which looked quite good. 'I've hidden the green food colouring though,' he said, which made us both smile.

For the front garden Mum has covered the four old toilet seats with silver foil and put a new inflatable alien in the middle of them. The toilet seat 'spaceship' doesn't look too bad because she's put a large foil-covered piece of card in the middle, which gives it a kind of flying saucer shape.

SOOOOOO EXCITED ABOUT TOMORROW NOW!

<u>**Sunday, 19th July**</u>
THE PARTY WAS A SUCCESS!
PARTY NEWS

Yesterday's Planetarium show was really good. We all lay back looking up at the stars. It felt exactly like we were outside.

After that Dad drove us home, and as we approached the house everyone saw the alien in the garden.

'Wow!' shrieked Holly, pointing at it.

'That looks very realistic,' said Sarah.

'So cute,' said Mandy.

We ran into the house and everyone rushed around, looking at the decorations. We had a party tea and a slice of alien cake before I opened my presents.

I got...

A remote control UFO from Sarah

A space projector lamp that shines stars onto the ceiling from Holly
And...
Shiny black pyjamas with gold stars on them from Mandy.

Before bed we watched a movie about a boy who keeps an alien in his sock drawer. (Number three in the 'sock drawer' series - quite good). Then we lay in my room looking up at the little stars coming out of the projector light, we watched them slowly moving around the room until we all fell asleep.

Wednesday, 22 July

Today Mandy's mum took us to a theme park to celebrate Mandy's birthday. It was brilliant, although I got very wet on the log flumes, which wasn't quite so good. After that we all went back to Mandy's house and helped her pack her FOUR suitcases ready for going to America. I'd got her quite a good present. It was like a lava lamp but full of glitter. It was from the same place we got the inflatable alien. (My new favourite shop.)

Sunday, 26th July
THE TRAVEL HOTEL

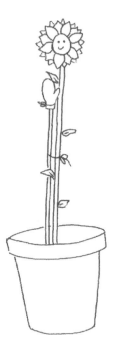

'Come on, it's time to go,' called Mum. We all piled into the car and set off for the Travel Hotel. I couldn't believe it…. I'd paid for the hotel and I held my chin up high as I opened the car window and felt the air rushing against my face.

On the way we drove past Mr Alimo's house and saw Mr Alimo and Grandma Merle sitting on the garden bench. Next to them was a pot with a huge flower in it. It took me a minute to realise that it was MY SUNFLOWER!

We drove to the Birmingham Travel Hotel. As soon as we got there we ran into the room and threw ourselves onto the large beds with their lovely white duvet covers. We all got into our pyjamas, ordered room service and watched a movie in bed. It was the best holiday ever.

Wooooooohoooooo!

HAPPY SUMMER!

If you liked this book, you might enjoy my other books about Maggie.

Maggie Moore and the Secret School Diary

Maggie Moore Wants to Win